BLIND MAGIC

NATALINA REIS

For information, contact the publisher, Hot Tree Publishing.
WWW.HOTTREEPUBLISHING.COM

EDITING: HOT TREE EDITING
FORMATTING: RMGRAPHX
COVER DESIGNER: CLAIRE SMITH

ISBN-13: 978-1-925655-30-8

10 9 8 7 6 5 4 3 2 1

*This book is dedicated to all my redheaded friends:
my sister, Marilia, and my friends Tammie, Nicole,
Guinevere, and Janna. Gingers rock!*

PROLOGUE

OLIVER

"Can you decide already?" It was taking an inordinate amount of time for Marc to pick out a card. He scratched his head and played with a couple of short red strands of hair in deep concentration, as if trying to come up with the solution to a quantum physics problem. "Jesus, Marc. I'm getting white hair just sitting here waiting."

My friend raised his eyes to mine and frowned. "Can you shut the fuck up so I can focus?"

I put my cards down and rested my head on the table for a moment while my complicated friend stared at his cards for the hundredth time. An outside noise made me snap to attention and tune everything else out. I heard it again—a muffled gasp and steps. Yes, I could most definitely hear stealthy steps approaching, the sound of snapping branches and crunched-up leaves reaching my fine-tuned ears. I put a finger to my lips to signal Marc and he jumped into action, his hand going directly to his holster. I followed suit and we quietly moved away from the table and positioned ourselves by the window. I waved a finger at Marc, letting him know I was going to take a quick scan of whatever was going on outside.

It was probably nothing, but it was never a bad idea to be cautious.

Outside, nothing moved besides the leaves in the breeze. *Did I imagine it?* I looked at my partner, who was cautiously peeking outside too. He shook his head. We waited a few more minutes, keeping our eyes glued to the trees and bushes whose branches mockingly waved and danced in the wind. No movement. We holstered our guns and let out a sigh of relief.

We had been keeping these two witnesses safe from the mobster trying to get to them. It hadn't been easy. Not because their hideaway had been uncovered, but because the two lovebirds argued constantly, and the girl had a penchant for unplanned jogs in the woods. They seemed to be very unwilling to be cooped up together and had no trouble letting everybody know it. They were not fooling me. I had seen the yearning looks the male, Jeremy Peter, threw at her when she wasn't looking. And Emily Rose had been a little too attentive when he had twisted his ankle a few days before for someone who apparently didn't care.

"Fucking trees!" Marc was not one to mince words. I laughed. We both sat back down to resume our card game. "Now I can't remember what I was going to play."

I didn't have time to groan about my friend's renewed indecisiveness. The door to the mother-in-law suite we were staying in slammed open and two hulks dressed in camo with faces covered by balaclavas burst through it. Our reaction was immediate, but not fast enough. By the time we had jumped to our feet, guns in our hands, the two men had their firearms pointed at us.

"Drop the guns." The muffled voice left no doubt as to his intent.

We raised our hands up in surrender. In my head—and I'm sure Marc's too—a plan to take them down before they got to our charges was already percolating. If we worked together, we could theoretically get the upper hand, even though their guns were bigger and much more impressive than ours.

"Last chance. Drop the fucking guns."

Almost in unison, my partner and I slowly deposited the guns on the floor in front of us. Part of me wished that our lovebirds had heard the racket caused by their arrival, and run. The other half hoped they didn't for fear they would come bursting in on us and be killed instantly. These guys were not playing cops and robbers. Their weapons were military grade, and the muscles I could see were those of well-toned, extremely well-trained soldiers.

"Kick them over here." We obeyed.

I was hoping they would come over to tie our hands, so we could turn the tables on them. Instead, one of them pulled a handgun out of his pocket and pulled the trigger.

Marc went down first. It all happened too fast, but I

could see everything taking place in slow motion. My fellow cop went down on his knees, a thick, red shower exploding from his chest as a scarlet stain spread on his white shirt. I watched, as if from outside myself, as he dropped flat on the floor, eyes closed, his head bouncing off the wooden floor as if it was a basketball. My eyes turned to the gun now pointing at me. The sudden pressure of a bullet going through my skin, flesh, and bone at the speed of a locomotive pushed me backward, my feet nearly flying off the ground. I tried to yell but I gurgled instead and tasted blood. I was suffocating. My sight became blurry and my legs went numb beneath me. I looked down at my chest and stared in morbid wonderment as my own blood gushed out. My life was oozing out with it, one heartbeat at a time.

Like Marc, I fell first to my knees and then, face first, on the hard floor. No time to warn the innocent couple in the adjoining cottage. Proud as I was of being a cop who had never lost anyone under my protection or command, I had failed miserably that day—losing both a colleague and my charges. A terrible and dishonorable way to die.

Dust Bunnies & Blue Eyes

MARCY

"Nice bunnies, it's time to go." I often muttered to myself or things around my shop. It made for a less lonely day to hear my own voice. The dust bunnies seemed to be imitating their live namesakes and were reproducing at an alarming pace. I wiped under the shelf with an enthusiasm rivaled only by my eagerness to finish the task and have a good cup of Oolong tea. The Polka Dots and Eye of Newt witchcraft shop was not exactly busy these days. I had my loyal customers who always came back for more, but getting new ones seemed to be an issue. So when I heard the telling sound of my door chimes echoing through the shop, my heart almost skipped a beat with surprise.

A man and a woman waited by the register. I didn't recognize them.

New customers!

They hadn't seen me yet so I had the chance to study

them while I approached from the back of the store. The woman was tall and gorgeous with beautiful long, dark hair that fell in cascades of silkiness down her shoulders and back. She held herself slightly apart from the man, looking around her with a tightness around her mouth that could only mean she didn't like what she saw. The man looked familiar but I couldn't place him. Handsome and standing at least one foot taller than me, hair just as dark as the woman's but cropped very short in an almost military cut. Both were dressed elegantly in conservative suits, as if they had arrived from a business meeting somewhere. The man didn't move much, staring ahead, apparently interested in whatever was displayed on the shelf behind the counter. *Weird*. There was nothing but an empty shelf there.

As if suddenly aware I was watching, the man glanced over at me. I stumbled backward, teetering on my high heels and overcome with an emotion I couldn't explain. My heart raced at the speed of light, assailed by images of me and the stranger. Heat ran through me, frizzing my hair and curling my toes as vivid memories of his lips moving over mine took over all my senses.

I don't even know the guy. How can I remember his taste?

But I could. I could taste coffee and dark chocolate, life and happiness, heaven. My body tingled in anticipation and pleasure as I recalled how his hands had cupped my breasts, enticingly warm and eager—

What the hell?

I could almost hear the crackling of fire, the eruption of feelings long forgotten, and the overwhelming yearning for a man who felt so familiar and yet, was but a stranger. *Something's coming this way*— I forced myself to snap out of whatever this was and stepped forward.

"Welcome to the Polka Dots and Eye of Newt!"

My greeting startled the woman enough that she swiveled to look at me, but the man barely moved, acknowledging my arrival only with a slight nod. For a moment—a tiny fraction of a moment—I worried I would scare them away with my eccentric ways. Throughout the years I had found that people were a bit put off by my loud sense of style and odd choice of accessories. The moment past, I focused on making the newcomers feel at home.

"What can I do to help you? There is a potion and a spell for every ailment." I giggled at my own statement. "I just can't bring back the dead."

The stunning woman wrinkled her nose as if she had smelled something bad, and licked her red, generous lips. Her gray aura was covered in an overlay of bubbly yellow— joy, slightly marred by guilt maybe. "Are you Marcy, the witch?"

"My reputation precedes me, I see." I laughed again as I came around to the back of the counter. "So what can I do for you today?"

"I feel a little weird asking this, but…." The woman looked around as if afraid she would be overheard. I stole a glance at the man, still standing and staring stoically at the very empty and totally uninteresting shelf behind me. "Do you have something to help Oliver?" She looked at the man next to her. He twitched a little, the corners of his mesmerizing blue eyes crinkling.

"I'm assuming you're Oliver." I pointed at the man, but he didn't move. A wave of electricity coursed through my body, and I shivered. "Help you with what exactly?"

"Is there a more private place to talk?" *Lord, really?* The shop was empty. It didn't get much more private than this. *The customer is always right.* I pointed toward my small lounging area where a couple of overstuffed armchairs and a sofa surrounded a bright, tile-top coffee table.

The woman looped her arm through Oliver's and they both followed me into the seating area. "Would you like some tea?" God, I hoped they did. My stomach was begging me for the comfort of its heat and tangy flavor.

"No, thanks." Why wasn't Oliver saying anything? And why did she help him to the chair? He was fully grown—and beautifully so, if I was honest with myself—and seemed to be totally capable of sitting himself down without any help. I sat next to the woman. "My name is Eva Dawson. This is my brother, Oliver." She licked her lips again and placed her hands on her lap, her legs crossed at the ankles. She was the living picture of decorum and elegance. "Oliver is a policeman. You may remember him from about a year ago when he was shot while protecting two witnesses."

"Of course!" I remembered now. No wonder he looked familiar. He was one of the cops who had been shot while on protection detail for my friends, Em and Jem. Not that it explained the connection I felt with him. "How are you doing, Oliver? You look like you've recovered well." Oliver's eyes twitched again but didn't quite turn to me, choosing instead to stare at the wall.

Look at me, fool.

The yearning for his attention overshadowed everything else.

Look at me, please.

I shook my head, trying to dispel those feelings and focus on the matter at hand. Back then, Emily Rose and Jem had been taken to a safe house in the middle of nowhere, and two police officers, one of whom was now dating my friend Celia, had been assigned to be their guards. Things had turned sour and their location was unveiled to the criminals who were after them. Two cops were shot and my friends kidnapped before things normalized again. I vaguely remembered Oliver from the pictures in the news.

"During surgery, there were some complications and Oliver had to be resuscitated." The beautiful woman stole a glance at her brother. "The doctors think that the trauma to his heart caused the problem."

I stared at the elegant woman, waiting for her to continue. Caused what problem? Oliver didn't seem to be suffering from any visible ailment. "What problem are we talking about?"

Eva opened her mouth to answer, but for the first time since they had arrived at the shop, Oliver spoke instead. "Hallucinations. I suffer from frequent and disturbing hallucinations." There was a sharp edge to his voice as his eyes turned to me. "Hard to be a cop when you are being controlled by imaginary foes."

I was quiet for a moment. He was right, of course.

Doing the work he did under the duress of being ravaged by hallucinations could not be easy or safe for anyone involved.

"While I was in the hospital I heard stories about you, Ms. Spellman." His sister seemed now content to let him explain. "There were stories about how one of your potions actually helped save the young couple we were protecting."

I fidgeted on my seat, my glasses sliding down my nose and perching precariously on the tip. "It was a simple sleeping potion. You smell it, you fall asleep." Nothing that could cure an illness. "Are you asking me to come up with something to cure your condition?"

Oliver Dawson burst out laughing. For the first time his facial muscles relaxed and his handsome face, covered in a day-old stubble, opened up. "God no!"

I glanced at Eva for clarification. Was I missing something?

"We know you can't cure his head trauma," she explained, throwing her brother a worried glance. Oliver was still laughing. "We were wondering whether you'd have a potion to ease these episodes though."

I looked at Oliver. He was a very handsome man. Very much not my type with his clean-cut black hair, classical style, and gorgeous blue-gray eyes. Hell, who was I kidding? He was every woman's type. "What exactly do you see?" His eyebrows arched slightly. "I need to know what type of hallucinations you are having to come up with an antidote of sorts."

Oliver licked his lips—and what luscious lips he had—and hesitated for a second as if searching for the right words.

"They start as blobs of different colors—vivid and bright—and normally develop into bizarre malformed shapes that grow and fade."

His voice, however cool, and a repetitive drumming of fingers on his leg betrayed a level of anxiety that didn't match his demeanor. When he lifted his gray-blue eyes to mine, I buckled under the weight of a crushing sense of helplessness. His aura was a shade of sulfur—a sign of pain deep inside him, the kind of guarded pain no one can see but that eats you from the inside out.

He cleared his throat and wiped his brow with a hand. "Well?"

Yeah, I had a tea that would most definitely help alleviate the intensity of his hallucinations, if not make them fade away completely. "It will be ready for pickup by tomorrow afternoon. I will be glad to deliver it, if you'd like."

Eva didn't let Oliver refuse the offer. "That would be great. I have a court case tomorrow and I'm not sure I would be able to drive you here, Oliver." She handed me a business card. "Here's my brother's address and phone number."

"I'll be at work tomorrow." He was not driving—possibly because of his hallucinations—so did that mean he was on desk duty only? I didn't know much about jobs in law enforcement other than what I watched on TV, but I gathered it was normal for a policeman to be taken out of the field after a traumatic experience. "Unless you want to deliver it to the precinct." His voice spoke volumes more. He did not want me to go there. I wondered why. "We can come and pick it up later in the week."

Not a quitter, I stood my ground. "Absolutely not. I will be glad to deliver it to your workplace. Which precinct is it?" I almost laughed at the expression of disappointment and annoyance on his face.

A few minutes later, Oliver wrapped a black-and-white chevron scarf around his neck and, holding on to his sister's arm, made it clear he was ready to leave. "Thank you, Ms. Spellman. You've been very kind." He reached out with his free hand in a gesture of polite dismissal.

"Please call me Marcy." I had a sudden urge to touch him, so I slipped my hand inside his and shook it. Startled, he flinched, but held my hand in a firm grasp. "Very nice to meet you, Oliver. You too, Eva. I will see you tomorrow."

They left, but the feeling of his warm hand lingered in mine. So did the fear I'd felt coming from within him. It wafted up in the air like a staggering perfume, one that takes your breath away—not in a good way. He may have been strong but the hallucinations he was having scared him to death. I had never met him before, but the wish to help him was oddly strong.

As soon as they left the store I retired to my small lab—a kitchen really, but calling it a lab gave it more substance—to concoct the tea I was hoping would alleviate his hallucinatory spells. If you knew your herbs well, it was possible to find something to help with pretty much any ailment. It wouldn't cure anything, per se, but it would definitely make it a lot more bearable.

After the strange—but delicious—visions I'd had earlier, I was very much looking forward to delivering it to him the next day.

OLIVER

"Quirky little thing." My sister often found it hard to accept that not everyone was as perfect as her. Eva had always been beautifully put together with the body of a model, the brains of a rocket scientist, and the class and style of a classic Hollywood star. Very few people could compare themselves to her and come out the winner. "Do you think she'll really be able to help you?"

I smiled, the lavender scent of the witch still lingering in my nose. "I think she will definitely help me."

She was already helping me and probably totally unaware of it. Her voice had caressed my ears with the softness of a feather and the sweetness of honey. Marcy was soft-spoken even though unconventional in her style—or so Eva thought. Her voice was like a balm for my broken heart. And her hair! Bright red, as if her locks were ablaze. So bright even I couldn't miss it.

"How can you be so sure? She's a tiny little thing with all that red, out-of-control hair, and those glasses! Lord, those glasses are something to behold." I laughed. Eva would first be caught dead rather than wearing glasses of any kind. Even though she had had bad eyesight since she was about fifteen, she never once had worn the diabolical contraptions, as she liked to call them. For my perfect sister, it had always been contacts.

"Marc's dating her best friend. He swears she's the

real thing. You know Marc. He's a no-nonsense, as real and grounded as you can get kind of guy." The car swerved suddenly to the right and I hit my head on the window. "Ouch! Watch where you're going. Are you trying to kill me because I made you go to a witchcraft store?"

"Sorry. This guy cut me off." Eva wouldn't curse, not even when she was pissed off. She took a deep, audible breath to calm herself down. "Maybe she is all that, but she is a bit…" I could almost hear her sharp brain looking for the right words. "Weird. There, I said it. She was wearing the most god-awful clothes I have seen in a long time. Loud and oddly matched."

I laughed again, rubbing the bump on my head. "Not everyone has your amazing sense of style, sis. That doesn't make her weird. Just different from you."

Eva was driving me to work. Since the shooting I had to rely on others to get to where I needed to go. Marc often gave me a ride in the morning, since he lived in the same neighborhood, but I'd wanted to visit Marcy's store this morning. I was surprised when Eva volunteered. She was not the most demonstrative person in the world, but I knew she loved me more than she led me to believe. I also knew she was a lot more generous than she wanted everyone to think. Eva was a complicated woman with so many defense mechanisms, I often thought of her as some kind of mechanical princess worthy of a steampunk novel. But inside that metal, cold shell there was a warm heart that beat and bled like everyone else's.

"Do you need me to pick you up after work?"

For the first time in months, Eva had a day off, and I was not about to ruin it for her any more than I already had. "No, I'll get a ride or call a cab. You enjoy your day off." She didn't talk much about her private life, not even with me. I knew she dated once in a while, but the details of such events were kept as protected as a national treasure. "Are you going on a date?"

"Now you're just being nosy." I had hit a nerve. "What if I am?"

Yes, there it was; the prickly shield. Growing up with our parents had not been easy and had left us both with certain scars. "That would be great. I want you to be happy."

"Sorry." Her voice softened. "I didn't mean to snap at you. I do have a date this evening. No big deal. We haven't known each other for long."

"I'm glad you have someone in your life." We left it at that as the car slowed down and finally stopped. "Thank you for taking me to the witch, sis. I truly appreciate it."

"You're welcome. If this tea helps you with your hallucinations I will personally hug the witch." The uncharacteristically humorous comment made me laugh again. I was experiencing a totally new side to my sister today. "I'll come around to open the door. We're right in front of the precinct."

Eva had parked in the special parking place reserved for the captain. She was the only one who could get away with it. Men often had trouble getting mad at my sister. "Don't get out. I can manage. Thanks again, and I'll see you later."

I wished her a fun date and ambled my way to the door,

almost crashing into a passerby. I was greeted inside by the usual chorus of friendly voices wishing me a good morning. Nothing like being injured to bring the friendliness out of your fellow cops. I made my way through the obstacle course that was the main room of the precinct into my office. With the door closed behind me, I dropped into my comfortable chair and closed my eyes. I could still smell her, all lavender and spices, a voice that soothed my nerves, and skin as soft as velvet. As we said our goodbyes and her hand found its way into mine, I'd felt something I hadn't in a long time. A warm tingling had coursed through my veins and made me shiver in delight. This little witch might be just what the doctor ordered.

Tea & Old Scotch

MARCY

My breath was coming out in giant puffs of white. Winter was coming early. Barely into fall and the temperatures were already too frigid for even the autumn flowers to remember it was time to bloom. I tucked the edges of my pink-and-orange woolen coat together and blew a couple times onto my hands to bring some feeling back to them as I dismounted from my bike. With my car in the shop, my faithful bike was my only mode of transportation. Stupid to ride a bike in this cold weather, but the precinct was too far for walking and I didn't feel like waiting for the bus. Nothing against public transportation, but I always seemed to sit next to someone who hadn't changed his socks in weeks. My nose, used to the exotic smells of my potions and teas, couldn't handle a long stinky ride any more than I could eat acid.

I parked my purple-and-pink bike in the small bike

parking stand in front of the station, rubbed my hands together a few more times, and walked in through the front door of the precinct. An almost uncomfortable blast of hot air hit me straight in the face as I crossed into the main lobby. It was a small but busy place. Our little town was what some people used to call a one-cop town. Even though that wasn't true anymore, it was still a small enough place to have equally small police stations.

The middle-aged police officer standing behind the counter that ran across most of the lobby looked up at me with curious eyes. I watched her eyes open up as she took me in. I often received that reaction. I knew I was a bit eccentric in the way I dressed, but I could never quite understand why people couldn't handle it a bit more gracefully. In spite of it all, I caught myself ironing out imaginary creases on my beautifully striped coat as I approached her.

"I'm looking for Officer Dawson." *Or is he a detective? Do detectives get called officers as well?* I realized I knew very little about law enforcement. Maybe I should've been a little less law-abiding in my early years and got acquainted with the men—and women—in blue.

The woman, her eyes still a bit dazed, scanned me from head to toe as if wondering what someone like me could ever have to do with lovely, classic, clean-cut Oliver Dawson. "May I ask what you want with him?" Who was she? Oliver's mother?

"I came to deliver something he ordered from me yesterday. Is he in?" I looked around the room, searching for his handsome figure, but couldn't find him.

She hesitated for a moment. "Yes, his office is in the back to the left. His name is on the door." Standing up, she walked around her perch on the counter to open a small old-fashioned swinging gate to let me in. "Can I have your name for the visitors' registry?"

"Marcy Spellman." Not stopping to see if she'd got it, I headed decisively to the back where I could see a few offices. I found his right away. It was the only one that had a closed door and a rather large sign at eye level with his name in three-dimensional letters. I knocked, a little nervous all of a sudden. "Mr. Dawson? Oliver?"

The muffled sound of his voice came through the door and I opened it in spite of not being sure he'd actually told me to. Oliver sat at an old dark-wood desk, headphones draped around his neck, dark hair impeccably combed back and an expression of curiosity in his sexy eyes. "Yes?"

"It's me, Marcy." I wasn't sure why I was announcing my presence, since I was obviously there and it wasn't as if he had forgotten what I looked like from the day before. I bit my lip. I was never this nervous around people. What was it about this man that made me so jittery?

His amazing blue eyes lifted toward me and my stomach dropped a few inches. I could see eternity in those eyes.

"I have your tea."

Duh! What else would I be here for? It wasn't as if we were friends or anything. With a start, I realized I wanted to be. I wanted to be someone who had a steady role in his life. *Knock it off, dummy. You just met him yesterday.*

For the first time since he'd walked into my store, a

smile stretched across his lips, leaving me breathless. Was that how he got confessions from the prisoners? Because I'd confess whatever he wanted me to at that moment. Memories of the visions I'd had before made me tremble, desire spreading through me like wildfire.

"Ms. Spellman, good to see you again." *Is it?* He hadn't been that friendly the day before. "I wanted to apologize for my behavior yesterday. I was in a very gloomy mood and I'm afraid I was probably rude to you."

My lips twitched but the smile wouldn't come. Instead, I fixed a lock of my hair that had come loose from the bun on top of my head. *I must look a fright.* He was so elegant, so put together. I—well, not so much. For a moment I wished I looked different.

"You were not rude." He wasn't. Maybe a little too serious and too anxious to get out of my store at the end. But not rude.

"Please sit down." He pointed at a chair next to his desk. The thought of refusing it never crossed my mind. Gingerly I sat on the edge of the wooden chair and licked my lips nervously. "So, any luck with the tea?"

"Yes, of course. The tea." I had forgotten why I was there. *What is going on?* I pulled a small container from my purse and placed it on top of the desk, in front of him. "Two teaspoons in hot water. Let it steep for two minutes, strain it, and then drink it. You can sweeten it if you like. The herbs are a little tart."

His hands fumbled a little over the desk before taking hold of the tin. He opened it and took a whiff. His nose wrinkled in a rather comical way. "Holy shit! What's in this? It smells like something crawled and died in here."

I burst out laughing. It was a pretty on-the-nose description of the smell. The herbs I had used reacted to each other by letting off a very rotten smell. The tea wouldn't taste as bad as it smelled though. "Yeah, not the nicest-smelling tea I ever put together, but effective. Drink it three to four times daily."

Oliver replaced the cover on the canister and dropped it in a drawer of his desk. "How much do I owe you?"

The dreaded question. I was running a business, but I hated charging for things people needed. If he had bought a necklace as a novelty for his girlfriend—who I was very much hoping didn't exist—or scented oils for the house, I wouldn't have any trouble charging him, but medicinal stuff?

"Why don't we wait to see if it works first? Then I will charge you."

That gorgeous smile I had seen before made another appearance. "That hardly seems fair. Let me at least buy you a cup of coffee."

I scanned the room around me. "From the kitchen here? This precinct looks fresh out of an eighties police drama. I bet they have an old Mr. Coffee machine somewhere, right?"

Oliver laughed. "Actually we have a very modern, state-of-the-art espresso machine. But you're right. This precinct hasn't seen any changes in decor since the early nineties." He slapped the top of the desk playfully. "But I was really inviting you to a coffee out in town. Or tea, if you prefer."

Be still my beating heart. "That would be lovely, thank you. Yes, tea is more my speed." The excitement growing inside my chest was almost choking me. The sense of familiarity and intimacy I felt around him was as absurd as it was thrilling, pregnant with promise and possibilities.

"Are you available in an hour or so? My shift will be over and we can go next door to the Caffeine Corner." Even if I wasn't, I would *make* myself available. Coffee or tea with the swoon-inducing Officer Dawson was well worth waiting for.

I agreed and told him I would wait for him there. I didn't have time to go back to the store, so I might as well sit in the coffee shop and read for a while. In my bag I carried at least one hundred books—e-books, that was. As much as I loved the feeling of a real paper copy in my hands, it was a lot easier to carry them in electronic format. I often bought both the e-copy and the paperback. Books, like my herbs and crystals, were very important to me. Not many people knew that I was a closet romance fan—in fact, I believed only Celia was aware. There was something about a good love story that made you feel all oozy and beautiful inside. The idea that there was indeed someone out there who was your soul mate, your other half, was too attractive for me to dismiss as a fantasy. Deep down inside I believed—hoped— that there was someone out there for me too. I pulled my reader out of my purse and settled in a small booth, a cup of steaming Oolong tea on the table in front of me.

Buried under the romantic avalanche of my book, I didn't notice Oliver until he was standing right by my table, a cute waitress holding on to his arm.

"Earth to Ms. Spellman." The playful tone in his voice was too endearing for words. His conservative looks contrasted sharply with his voice, and I couldn't help but smile like an idiot.

"Mr. Dawson. Sorry. I was deep into my book." From where I was sitting, he looked like a giant, towering over everybody and everything. I waved at the seat across from me. "Please, sit down."

The girl, still hanging on to his arm as if her life depended on it, looked adoringly at him. "Just call me if you need me, Oliver."

Over my dead body, girl. He was all mine right now. The visions told me so. She better crawl back to whatever preschool she came from and leave me alone with the gorgeous man in blue—even if he was wearing an impeccable, expensive-looking black suit.

Oliver sat and, looking up at his groupie, smiled. I could have sworn the sun had descended on the cozy little coffee shop. "Thank you, Dory. See you later."

The starry-eyed young woman turned and left, but not before giving me a dirty look. *Well, I don't like you either.* I was immediately ashamed of my reaction. I couldn't even remember the last time I had cared about anyone stealing a guy's attention from me. But I was drawn to Oliver like a magnet to the poles. Something about this man had turned my dormant heart into an exploding volcano. Not to mention all the other girly parts.

"Baby sister?" I couldn't help it. Men were always

so oblivious to obvious age gaps between them and their admirers.

"Dory?" She was so young her parents had named her after the cartoon fish. *Now you're just being mean.* "She works here and she's always been very kind to me." With those blue eyes, what self-respecting girl wouldn't be?

"She's head over heels in love with you." *Oh my God! What's wrong with me?* He laughed in a self-deprecating fashion. "No. Really. I'd recognize that expression of undying adoration anywhere." Still talking? Could I just shut up once and for all?

With a chuckle, he leaned slightly over the table, stretching his forearms on the top. "I've known her since she was a kid." She *was* a kid! *Shut up, shut up.* "So, Ms. Spellman, what would you like to drink?"

A glance inside my mug told me my tea had gone cold long ago. "Oolong would be nice." Oliver waved a waiter over and ordered my tea and a large coffee for himself. "Thank you for doing this, but it really wasn't necessary."

His fingers were interlaced and his eyes, a little unfocused, seemed to shine like gemstones in the dim space. "I think it was. You didn't have to hand deliver it." *But I did.* Well, at least I did if I wanted to see him again. So it was not an altogether altruistic act. "Has anyone ever told you, you have the sweetest voice?" Red alert! Red alert! My face was on fire. "It's like smooth, dark chocolate with a hint of delicious coffee." *Hell. Did it get really hot in here?*

"Mr. Dawson, I didn't take you for a flatterer." Not sure how I was able to talk, considering my throat had closed completely. "I'd be grateful if you kept me up-to-date on your progress. I may have to adjust the concentration of the tea."

The smile he gave me was brilliant. "Please, call me Oliver. Mr. Dawson's my father, and he's not known for being very nice."

We sat companionably, cradling our hot brews in our hands and making small talk for a while. A furtive glance at my watch told me I better get moving. Polka Dots and Eye of Newt was unmanned, and even though I'd left some protective wards in the shape of several onyx stones in each corner of the shop, I knew better than to leave it alone for too long. "Unfortunately, I've got to go. Oliver, it was a pleasure to meet you again. I hope my tea helps with your problem." I stood up, immediately followed by him. "Please, keep in touch."

Oliver smiled again. "I certainly will, Marcy." There was a promise in his voice. "I certainly will."

I left the coffee shop with an idiotic smile glued to my face. I couldn't help myself. Oliver Dawson seemed to have some weird power over me and, being a witch, that kind of power engendered not only respect but also a strong, overwhelming attraction. Dory might be too young and starry-eyed for him, but I hoped I was not.

OLIVER

"What kind of spell did you put on me, little witch?" Just like in the old song, Marcy seemed to have bewitched me somehow. Try as I may, I just couldn't take my mind off her. I'd sat at that table in the coffee shop for a good half hour after she left, smiling like a fool and incapable of moving. Now at home, I was still under her spell. I sat on my couch, my head full of images of a beautiful red-haired witch and my heart brimming with a new hope. Was it possible I could feel like that after all this time? Feel this strange pleasurable ache inside me, making me shiver in anticipation of what may happen? It had been so long since I felt anything like that.

A loud knock echoed through the house, snapping me out of my daydream. Why didn't people ever ring the bell? It was a lot easier on my ears. Ever since my surgery I'd become extremely sensitive to noise. I pressed the intercom button by the door. "Who's there?"

"It's me, you idiot. Did you forget you told me I could come over?" Marc had called earlier when I was still at work and asked if I was up for a nightcap and some manly talk—his words, not mine. As soon as I opened the front door, Marc strode into the apartment, slapping my arm as a greeting. "You need some real man time."

I chuckled and followed him to the couch. "Real man time spent with another guy? No offense, dude, but I was thinking more in terms of someone a bit bustier."

"I'm worried about you, Oliver, spending all your time alone in this dark, gloomy apartment." Marc helped himself to my small bar, the clinking and clanking of glass jarring to my ears. "Although… I hear you had a very attractive visitor at the precinct today."

I took the glass he held up to me and smelled it. Scotch. The expensive one I kept for special occasions. I smiled and took a sip. Even though I wasn't much of a drinker, I enjoyed the occasional good burn from a vintage scotch. "It was your friend Marcy."

Marc let out a choked sound. "What? Marcy? I should've guessed when someone mentioned she had a pink-and-orange-striped coat." He laughed and gave my knee a friendly slap. "You dog! Here I am, thinking you're not getting any and look at you!"

"For your information, you dirty-minded lout, I'm not getting any. I just met Marcy. She came to the precinct to deliver a tea I bought from her." I took a big gulp of the old scotch and savored the slow burn as it slid down my throat to my stomach.

"You speak like an eighty-year-old man. Too much education, not enough sense." Marc was the only friend who felt comfortable making fun of my overly educated background. "Fuck, what are you waiting for? Ask her out before you're too old to get it up."

I wanted to act outraged at his crass comments but I couldn't. Marc was an amazing friend who'd stuck by my side since we'd both been shot. "Do you kiss your mom with that mouth?"

"My mother was the daughter of a sea captain. I learned to talk like this from her." My friend leaned into me and whispered, "How long's it been?"

Easier to pretend I didn't know what he was talking about. "What are you talking about, man?" I could smell the scotch on his breath.

"Since you got some." Hell, he never stopped. "How long has it been since you last got laid?" Could this conversation get any worse?

I jumped to my feet and paced. "Come on, Marc. Ever since the shooting it hasn't been that easy to… you know, attract the other sex."

"Oh yeah, girls just don't find you attractive at all." I could sense him rolling his eyes as his sarcastic tone echoed in my rather empty living room. "It must be hard to find one willing."

"You're lucky your girlfriend's not here." I decided to go on the attack, considering my line of defense wasn't working. "She'd be pissed with your *machista* comments."

"My what? Sometimes it's like you speak another language, man." He laughed heartily and stood up to lay a hand on my shoulder. "All I'm saying, Oliver, is that you need to date again. It's been too long and you're using your condition as an excuse to shut yourself off from the rest of the world."

There was some truth to his words, but it was my past before the injury that really held me back. My history in the love arena wasn't very good. If I was honest with myself, it was actually scary. Being rich and attractive to the opposite sex wasn't always in your best interest. I was a walking example of that. The mere thought of dating again—or even a one-night stand—was terrifying. The fear was so strong it eclipsed all desire to, as my good friend so crassly put it, get laid.

"So, what do you say we go out bar-hopping and pick up some chicks?" Marc was still at it. His persistence was a strong suit of his, but it could also be very annoying.

"Shit, Marc. You're in a relationship." And a good one by the looks of it. I was happy for him but also a little jealous.

"I'm not talking about it for myself." His protest came out loud and clear. The outrage in his voice made me laugh. "For you, idiot. A little fuck can go a long way to heal your wounds." Spoken like the player he was not.

"I'm working tomorrow, man." The horrible tea Marcy had given me was brewed and waiting for me in the kitchen. Despite the foul smell, I looked forward to tasting it. Not just because I was hoping it would indeed dispel my hallucinations, but because it'd also bring memories of the little witch's visit this afternoon. The smell of lavender invaded my senses as palpably as if Marcy was standing beside me. Dreaming of the red-haired witch was a lot more attractive to me than going out and chatting up strangers at the moment.

"Damn, man! You're the rich, handsome guy with all the muscles. This carrot head wants to live vicariously through you, dude. You're crushing my dreams." Marc left, disappointed but resigned to the fact I probably would never be the player he hoped I'd be. In spite of myself and all my bad experiences with the gentle sex, I was feeling a resurgence of what felt a lot like hope. Hope of what, though?

Love Potions & French Food

MARCY

"I invoke thee, Aphrodite, goddess of love, so I can find my soul mate. I invoke thee, Aphrodite, goddess of love, so I can overcome my loneliness." My voice, albeit quiet, echoed through the store. In front of me I had lit three yellow candles around a pretty white one. The sweet scent of the rose petals I had strewn around wafted up to my nose. I inhaled deeply as I finished the incantation. "Such is my will."

The mint tea in the vintage teacup was still steaming hot when I brought it up to my lips, and I had the sudden urge to blow on it. *No, that will mess up my love spell.* I took tiny sips instead and then blew out the candles one by one. I never concocted spells for myself. It was frowned upon—by me at least. I was a witch with very high standards and expectations. But I'd been alone for a very long time. And Oliver Dawson had done something to my dormant heart. I wanted to be loved. I wanted *him* to love me.

Tea all gone, I started picking up the rose petals. These would be dried out for about a week and then scattered in the closest stream. The one that ran right behind the shopping strip would do nicely. I felt guilty. I should be casting spells for other people, not trying to help myself. Ever since I'd first laid eyes on the gorgeous and rather aloof Mr. Dawson, I hadn't been able to stop myself from wanting—no, needing some good loving in my life.

"It only works if it is really what you want." My usual advice for my customers wasn't needed this time. I so wanted this. I'd never been lovesick in my life, but I definitely was now. Shock didn't even begin to describe how I felt about the sudden love-flood drowning my heart. Everyone knew that Marcy, the witch, didn't fall in love that easy. *Well, tell that to my stupid heart.* I was most certainly "hooked." No denying it. How else would you explain this sudden urge to prepare a love spell for myself?

With my love spell finished, I brushed some imaginary dust from my blue polka-dot dress and clicked-clacked my way to the front of the store on my favorite pink stiletto shoes. I thought that if I was going to cast a love spell I might as well wear my Cinderella shoes. I turned the open sign around and unlocked the door. It was very unusual for me to close the store even for a few minutes, but I hadn't wanted any interruptions while I conjured up Aphrodite's favor. Outside, people rushed by my store, tucking their coat lapels closer to them while their tails flapped in the blustery winter wind. It looked—and smelled—like snow. We didn't get much snow in this part of the country—especially this early in the season—but I could almost feel it when it was coming. And it was indeed coming. I shivered.

The phone rang and I rushed to the counter. "Polka Dots and Eye of Newt." It was an automatic response. "Potions and spells for every ailment."

The voice from the other side made me teeter on my heels. Oliver! "Ms. Spellman, is that you?" I hadn't heard from him in over a week. Several times I'd almost called him, but thought better in the end. To hear his voice now, right after I had finished with my love spell, was a good sign. A very good sign indeed.

"Mr. Dawson, so good to hear from you again." Formality wasn't my thing, but it looked like it was his and I so wanted to please him.

"Please, we had this conversation already. Call me Oliver." And what a lovely name it was. It reminded me of a time gone by. A time when courtesy was still a common thing, when men pulled chairs out and held doors open for women. I may have been an independent, free-spirited female, but I couldn't find any fault in old-fashioned genteelness. "I was wondering if you were free?"

For you I am always free. Hold on! Where was this coming from? I'd always been a little ditzy, but this was getting ridiculous. "Free for what?"

"I was going to stop by and give you a report on my progress." That sounded heavenly. *Make him work for it, Marcy.* "Well?"

"Let me check my calendar." Bullshit. I had never in my life had a calendar of any sort. I did check for moon phases and the sort because it applied directly to a lot of my potions and spells, but other than that I rarely even checked the calendar on my phone. "It looks like I'm free today. Do you want me to meet you at the coffee shop?"

"Absolutely not." His voice was warm and deep, filling in spaces within me I didn't even know were empty. "I'll come to you at the store. You've gone way out of your way to help me already. Let's say in about an hour? I have to find a ride."

The next hour was a whirlwind of preparation—for what, I couldn't tell you. I couldn't stay still though. I swept an already spic-and-span floor. The dust bunnies all went into hiding when I produced my big, fluffy duster. I refilled my diffuser with lavender, and dabbed some of it behind my ears. When a young woman came in to purchase a crystal, I was so distracted I was almost sure I'd sold her the wrong one. And when my friend Celia called, I tried to dismiss her as fast I could.

"What the hell is going on, Marcy?" She wasn't one you could dismiss that easily. "First you leave me a message that you need to talk to me urgently, and now that I'm listening, you don't want to talk?"

"Sorry, Celia." It was true. I'd called her that morning to talk to her about this weird attraction I had for the most unlikely candidate for my heart. She'd been at the hospital working and couldn't talk to me then. "Oliver Dawson's coming over any minute and I'm all flustered."

"*The* Oliver?" I could almost see her eyes, big and round like saucers.

"Yes, one and the same." My eyes kept roaming toward the door, anxious and excited all at once. "I've never been this stupid about a guy. Never!"

Celia laughed in her usual funny snorts. "You're not being stupid. You're smitten."

"He's not even my type." Now I was whining. "He's all straitlaced and proper. I'm all—well, you know me; I'm all Marcy." I laughed along with her. Whatever people called me, straitlaced and proper was not it. "Why this man? And why now?"

"Marcy, my good friend, you once told me that when it comes to love there is no rhyme or reason." Celia knew me better than anyone else in the world. "That your heart picks whoever it wants, whenever, and there is nothing you can do about it."

I sighed loudly. She was right. I always said that to everyone who came to me with their love woes. In fact, I had said something along those lines to Celia's sister when she was fighting with her own heart. In the end her heart had won—as it usually did.

"You are the least judgmental person I know, Marcy." Celia's voice was quieter now. "Who is to say that just because he is very different from your usual free-spirited, unconventional type, he's not the right guy for you? Your soul mate?"

There was truth in her words. They filled my heart with a new hope and I felt myself relax a little. That was, until I saw

Oliver's tall and magnificent figure coming through the door. "Got to go, Celia. He's here."

I hung up the phone and watched as Oliver gingerly stepped inside the store, waving at someone I couldn't see. The door closed behind him and he froze. "Marcy! Are you here?"

Weird. I was standing just a few feet away from him and the store wasn't that dark. "I'm here, Oliver." I took a few steps forward and watched his face open up in a generous smile as his blue eyes followed my voice.

"Can you give me a hand here, please?" *With what?* "I'm not familiar enough with your store yet to navigate it on my own."

Not sure what he meant, I stopped shy of touching him when I noticed he was holding on to a thin, long cane. I froze for a second, processing this bit of new information.

"You're blind!" Tact had never been my forte. Unfortunately, I often had a hard time controlling my own mouth.

Oliver laughed, a great belly chuckle that reverberated throughout the space. "You're just now realizing that?"

Well, hell! He didn't look blind. His eyes followed light and my movements. "You didn't have a cane the last couple times I saw you."

"The first time I had my sister with me, and the second time Dory was there to give me a hand, so to speak." I was so ashamed! Here I was thinking that little Dory was holding on to him for less than savory reasons, and she was only helping him out. "I went blind after the shooting."

Snapping out of the half trance I was in, I held on to his elbow and guided him to the lounge. "I had no idea. Your eyes seem to follow and react to movement and light like everyone else's...." I sat next to him on the largest sofa, staring curiously at him and feeling guilty for doing it.

He was still chuckling, as if the fact I couldn't tell a blind man from a seeing one was very funny. "I have cortical blindness. When they had to resuscitate me, something happened to the part of my brain that connects to my eyes. I see light and even movement most of the time, but nothing else." His voice caught in his throat and I knew he was not as at ease with his condition as he would like me to think he was. "It also causes the hallucinations. Which are much better, by the way." His amazing cesious eyes latched on to mine as if he could see me. "Thank you so much." His hand covered mine and I realized I was still holding on to his arm.

"Right there. You just looked at me as if you could see me." Why couldn't I ever shut up?

"I don't know why, but I can see color—reddish—when you move." My freaking bright red hair! That had to be it. "You're easy to spot for some reason." I blushed, and for once I was glad he couldn't see it. Of all things to connect us in some way, my hair would not have been my first choice. I loved my hair, but it made me very visible the few times I would prefer to melt into the background.

Oliver told me how the tea I had given him had alleviated the hallucinations—or visual disturbances, as the doctors liked to call them—to a level that didn't interfere with his everyday life. He was now able to keep working, even if only on desk duty.

"What exactly can you do?" My lack of filter didn't bother me much normally, but in this case it did. In an unprecedented instance, I wished I was "normal." Man, I was in deep this time!

My lack of tact didn't seem to bother Oliver. "I'm still working on cases. With the help of special technology I can read—really, listen to—the case files and do investigative work from my desk. I just can't go in the field for obvious reasons." He smiled. "I think I've finally got to the point where my coworkers are not tiptoeing around me for fear of hurting my feelings or saying the wrong thing."

"Unlike me, who can't keep it in to save my life." And there it was again.

To my great surprise, Oliver leaned over and sought my hand. I hadn't moved it too far and had no trouble nudging it beneath his. The warmth of his palm seeped into my skin and made me shiver in pleasure. "I like your candor, Marcy. Very much." For the second time in the last few minutes, my cheeks burned with the intensity of a bushfire. "You just say it like it is and that is very refreshing."

His thumb caressed the palm of my hand and I lost control of my heart. I pulled away from him. "Well, you had me fooled completely." I rubbed my hand on my lap, trying to stop the tingling his touch had left behind. Did my voice hold a tone of hurt?

Oliver frowned. "I'm sorry. I never meant to mislead you." I knew that, but I did feel a little foolish not having realized it from the get-go.

Silence fell on both of us for a moment. "Would you like some tea?" I broke the awkward quiet and stood up, determined to do something—anything—rather than sit there feeling weird.

A beautiful smile illuminated his face. "Not another of your miraculous teas."

In spite of myself, I laughed. "No, just a simple Oolong, or Earl Grey if you prefer."

"Oolong for you." Was it wrong that I melted at the fact he remembered my preference? "I will give it a try. I don't think I even know what it tastes like. I'm a coffee guy, I'm afraid."

After I served the tea, we sat companionably sipping on the hot brew. Me, sighing in delight. Him, making funny faces and wrinkling his nose. "Don't like it?"

"Not sure. It is not a taste I'm familiar with." He continued sipping and, to his credit, never gave up despite the many strange grimaces he accompanied each sip with. I laughed, delighted by his reaction and plain happy to share this mundane experience with him.

"I can't imagine how it must have felt." My mouth took control again, even if I was barely aware of the thoughts in my head. "Waking up blind, I mean."

Oliver raised his eyes to me in that unsettling manner that was so uncharacteristic of someone blind. "I didn't quite wake up blind." His voice was steady. "I was at home one day a few weeks after my surgery, watching TV, and suddenly the images on the screen began to waver and blur, kind of like smoke from a blown-out match. It flickered in and out of focus until it began darkening. An hour later I could see the flickering of lights from the TV screen but I couldn't see any images."

"Were you alone?" My heart contracted at the thought of something like that happening and no one being around to help.

"Yes…." He trailed off, and I thought he was not going to elaborate. But I was wrong. "I was in a panic. My heart racing a million miles a minute, my hands shaking, and my mouth drier than a desert. I couldn't move. I literally sat on the couch in front of the TV for hours, not daring to move for fear of making it worse. All I could do was open and close my eyes, hoping that it would just go away." I longed to hold his hand, to comfort him. "My sister came and found me sitting there, staring blankly at the screen, pale and shaking. The rest is history."

"And the hallucinations?"

He put the now empty teacup down on his lap. "Apparently, they are common among sufferers of cortical blindness. It's your brain playing tricks on you." I took the cup from him and placed it on the table. "The doctors think that I may or may not regain my sight in time." He chuckled. "Not very helpful. I'm learning how to deal with it just in case I won't ever see again."

"Be glad you can't see me. I'm a fright right now." I was trying to make him laugh, but there was some truth to my words. I was very comfortable with who I was most of the time. I had decided a long time ago that it was futile to try and change to fit in. That said, sometimes I caught myself wishing for a less eccentric personality, one that may not stick out so much. Preferably one that wouldn't attract judgmental stares from others.

"With a voice like that, I can't believe it for a second." I blushed again, the heat rising to my cheeks making my eyes water. I reached out to the big blue bow holding my messy curls in a bun, as if to double-check it was still there. "I imagine you as a beautiful, elegant young woman with radiant red hair and—blue eyes?"

Other than the beautiful, elegant part he was pretty much on the money. "Depends on the day and mood. I'm a witch, remember? My eyes change from dark blue to violet, even brown sometimes when I'm feeling rather cranky." I was speaking the truth. Eye doctors had agonized over the mystery that was my eyes. Even though eyes often changed color, blue switching to brown was not in any way a common occurrence. Then again, I had always been a little different.

Oliver's face opened up in that gorgeous smile of his. "You must be very good at your witching job, because you have certainly bewitched me with just the sound of your voice." *Fire! Fire!* My face—and many other parts of my body—were on fire. "I'm so looking forward to getting to know you better."

I thought swooning was just something writers made up for romance novels, but I found out at that moment to be a very real thing after all.

OLIVER

"She really didn't know?" Eva's voice punctuated her words with a tinge of shock. "How could she not?"

We had met for lunch in her favorite restaurant, a tiny, sophisticated bistro on the outskirts of town. Chez Nicola was a French cuisine restaurant made famous by its temperamental but highly talented chef and owner. Nicola, the man, was often in the headlines because of arguments or outrageous comments he was known to make. The man had no filter but was an amazing cook.

I took a bite of my delicious shrimp croquettes. "I guess I'm very good at pretending I'm not blind." I chuckled softly, remembering Marcy's surprise when she realized I was indeed blind as a bat.

"Well, in her defense your eyes look absolutely fine." Eva defending another woman? I wasn't sure whether to be happy or frightened that my overly critical sister was siding with the little witch. "You seem to like her." It was a subtle question. Just as I didn't pry into her life, she was careful not to pry into mine either. If there was a silver lining to this blindness, it was the fact that we had got much closer since it happened. We were only two years apart, but our upbringing hadn't lent itself to a very tender, close sibling relationship. Our parents had made sure we competed with each other at every step of our lives, and it was only thanks to my illness that we had grown tired of it and learned to be true siblings.

"I do. There is something different about her." Not that

I could explain it. After all, I couldn't even see her past her red hair, which in itself was a wondrous thing. Hard to believe or explain why I could see the color of her hair when I couldn't see anything else.

Eva laughed. "Yes, she is definitely different." There was no criticism in her voice. Just a statement of fact. "Are you asking her out?"

Good question. The last time we'd seen each other, almost a week ago already, we had made no definite plans for a future date. I had implied I wanted to see her again, but what about her? Did she want to see me? Did she want to spend her time with a blind cop who had given up on love a long time ago? I was not often sorry for myself. I had bounced back from the darkness in my life. Determined to conquer all obstacles set in my way the day my eyes quit seeing, I'd fought and clawed my way back to the closest I could get to my previous life. My job—with some modifications—was given back to me in spite of my superiors' early trepidation. I lived on my own and was mostly independent from anyone else. But now, with Marcy looming on my horizon, doubt threatened to destroy my hard-won self-confidence. Would I be good enough for her to even consider dating me?

"I suppose I should." Who was I kidding? My pants felt tight and uncomfortable at the simple thought of her. There was no "suppose" about it. I was going to ask her out again. My body was begging me to, and it had been a long time since it had done that. The little witch had true magic if she could wake me up from my long dormant state. "Yes, I will ask her out."

"Is the tea working?"

"Now that you ask, I haven't had a single hallucination since I started drinking it." I'd been able to keep the horrible and debilitating visions at bay the whole week. "Marc was not kidding when he said she was good."

"How did my favorite police officer like his meal today?" Nicola's voice reached my ears like a blast of cold air. I had been so involved in my thoughts about Marcy, I had not heard him approach. So much for the sharp senses of the blind.

"It was delicious as usual," my sister answered for me while I regained my composure. Hard to do with the witch still on my brain. "You are an artist, Nicola." Kill them with flattery was always Eva's motto. "Flattery is like gold, only cheaper," she was prone to say.

"Yes, Nicola. It was a feast for the palate." I could play the game as well. Not that it was a lie. The food was fantastic and the croquettes I had just eaten were indeed amazing. I was not a foodie, but I did enjoy a well-prepared, creative meal. Nicola always delivered. "You spoil my taste buds." We all laughed.

Later in the car as we drove back home, Eva was unusually quiet. It worried me. Even though not a chatterbox, Eva had learned the art of casual conversation at a very early age and was normally the catalyst of a constant exchange of information when we were together. Now, she sat quietly at the wheel, and through her silence I could feel a certain level of tension. "What's going on, Eva?"

"You know, that's truly creepy when you do that. The knowing something is up even though you can't see me."

She giggled nervously, another sign she was trying to figure out how to tell me something I probably didn't want to hear. "Dad wants you to come over for dinner this weekend."

Despite their apparent innocence, those words were like daggers to my gut. "Hell no. I've told him before that those family gatherings were over for me." Anger mixed with anxiety filled my chest. My father and I were not on the best terms. Not now, not ever.

"Come on, Oliver. It's just dinner." Despite her words, I could hear the sympathy in her tone. "Just do it and get it over with. He's your father."

"Don't remind me." I cringed at my own words. As much as I couldn't stand my own father, he was my flesh and blood, and deep inside I still believed I owed him some respect and loyalty. "I don't want to listen to him lecturing me about my life. Just because I did not make the choices he wanted me to, does not make them bad or wrong."

"One hour, total." Eva, ever the lawyer, ever negotiating. "Give him an hour with the excuse you have an appointment, and I will get you out of there before Father can do any major damage to your fragile self-confidence."

I laughed at her choice of words. "Yes, definitely pretty frail." Sobering up, I licked my lips. "You know he's going to bring her up. I don't want to talk about Blake."

My sister was quiet for a moment. "I know. I'll do my best to deflect the conversation into one of my cases. Father can't resist discussing a high-profile criminal case." She was right about that. Nothing like the smell of a good fight in court and a hefty retainer. "Pretend it's a Band-Aid. Just pull it off once and for all." She was quiet again, the car slowing down around a curve. "Besides, if you don't I'll have to listen to him bitch about it forever, and I'll have to hire a hit man to kill you." Eva kept surprising me with her sudden sense of humor.

"All right, tell him we'll be there this weekend." I gave in. Maybe she was right. Get the painful filial dinner duty out of the way once and for all. I could always go to the gym afterward and get back at him with the punching bag. "One hour, Eva. No more." It was decided, but in my mind I was already imagining all kinds of excuses I could come up with not to go.

Caffeine & Indigestion

MARCY

"This Eye of Horus should do the trick." The squinting young woman reached out to touch the pretty silver amulet in the shape of an eye I had placed on the counter in front of her. "I have step-by-step instructions on how to perform the ritual to cleanse you from the effects of the evil eye in the bag. After you do the ritual, make sure you wear the Eye of Horus all the time to protect you from further danger." Handing her the small bag with the rock salt and the mustard seeds, I smiled to put her at ease. She looked so uptight.

The blond woman paid and thanked me, a small frown still on her lips. *You really need to lighten up, girl.* After all, we all knew that negative attitudes and thoughts attracted only bad things.

"Call me if the headaches and your neck are still bothering you afterward." She crossed the front doorway without as much as a wave or glancing back. I sighed. No potion, ritual, or amulet would do her any good if she didn't start being a lot more positive. Some people just seemed to bring it upon themselves.

My only other customer was busy in the novelty section picking pens in the shape of dragons for a friend's birthday. I sat on the high stool behind the counter and sighed again. My morning had been spent meditating in hopes it would calm my ever-growing lusty attraction to the very beautiful Mr. Dawson. I had sat on my hands—literally—the night before to prevent myself from calling and inviting him to my apartment. I had not felt like this in years. I dated often enough, but it was the go-to-dinner-kiss-goodbye or sometimes stay-the-night-kiss-goodbye type of dates. A little chemistry, but nothing to make my toes curl like the blind detective did with just a glance. Ironic, I know.

With a finger, I pulled my glasses up the bridge of my nose. I had started wearing glasses a few years ago when one of my contacts got lodged under my eyelid for longer than my nerves were able to handle. I decided then that glasses were the way to go until I could afford refractive surgery to fix my mild astigmatism. The only downside was the constant slip-downs on my very small nose. Otherwise I loved the stylish look my several pairs of eyeglasses added to my everyday outfits.

"I think I like this green one better than the red. What do you think?" The young man snapped me out of my reverie. He had two dragon pens in his outstretched hands and was looking at me as if he expected me to save him from certain death.

"That one." No need to hesitate. His aura begged for the green one. "Red would clash with your aura. That will be five bucks."

After lunch I found myself quite unexpectedly standing in front of Oliver's precinct. The plan had been to swing by the auto shop where my VW Beetle was ready for pickup, get my sweet yellow car, and return to the store for the afternoon rush. Okay, maybe I was overinflating the amount of business I normally got in the afternoon, but I did normally see a couple customers and God knew I needed the sales. Instead, I parked the Beetle on the street, slipped a few coins into the parking meter, and strolled all the way to the front door of what was quickly becoming a favorite place of mine. I stopped for a moment to look at the old building façade, and my stomach somersaulted. Now that I was there my courage seemed to have dissolved in the very cold air.

"Marcy, right?" The voice startled me awake. Dory stood beside me, her very young face open in surprise.

"Dory, what are you doing here?" She could ask the same of me of course, standing like a fool in front of the old building.

"I'm coming to pick up Oliver for lunch." My heart lurched. "I do it every day."

I was curious—or stalling. Not sure which. "How long have you been doing this? Have you known Oliver for long?" *Have you dated him?*

"I've known him since I started working at the coffee shop, when I was like fifteen. He always came in for lunch before the...." She paused for a moment. "Before the surgery. He was always very kind and took a real interest in all of us. He was different from the other customers, always asking us about our day and about our dreams and ambitions. Not just to make small talk. He really cared."

It didn't sound like they had dated. I sighed in relief. "And after the surgery?"

"He came back to work as soon as he could, but he couldn't go anywhere for lunch on his own." Dory hugged herself and I noticed for the first time that she was not wearing a coat. "One of his coworkers told me and I came to get him. I've been doing it ever since."

"That's very nice of you, Dory." It sure was. I felt bad for having had bad thoughts about her.

"Well, it's not totally unselfish." She giggled again, rubbing her hands on her arms. "He is so freaking hot, I love the looks I get when I am walking arm in arm with him." She winked at me and I had to laugh. "Why are *you* here?"

A short coughing fit overtook me. Yes, why was I there? "I was going to pay Oliver a visit, but then I thought he's probably busy." Bumbling idiot was what I was.

Dory giggled. "He would love it!" She sounded so sincere I wanted to hug her. "Listen, why don't you go and take him to lunch instead of me? I know he would get a kick out of a change of pace."

Despite my growing panic I got excited about the idea. "I don't know. He's expecting you."

"Bullshit! He's sick of me by now." She waved at a passerby. "You do it."

I gulped. "Okay, I'll do it." And die of embarrassment if he turned me down.

Dory smiled. "I better get back to work. See you in a few?" I nodded and she ran, waving at me before she disappeared around the corner.

After a deep breath, I made myself cross the threshold of the old building. The strange feeling of walking into the past hit me again. Only the computers and other gadgets strewn around kept the space grounded in the present. The same woman I had talked to my first time in the precinct was behind the counter. She raised her eyes to me and, surprising me, smiled.

Even though I was sure she knew exactly why I was there, I felt obligated to explain it. "I'm here to see Officer Dawson. Is he available?"

"Well, welcome back, Ms. Spellman." The female officer offered me another big smile and waved me to the swinging door. "You know where to find the detective. I'll sign you in." *Well, that's a little unsettling.*

As I made my way across the work space, I noticed all the glances and smiles I was receiving. What the hell had I done to deserve all the attention? However positive it seemed to be, it was just a bit nerve-wracking. I brushed my puffy black-and-white polka dot skirt, suddenly worried I looked like a loon—which was dumb, of course, considering Oliver couldn't see me. I had the ridiculous feeling I was the proverbial dead-man-walking in prison movies. *Stupid.* People were smiling, not frowning in pity.

At the end of that very long short walk I faced Oliver's

door with serious trepidation. Why were all those people smiling at me as if they knew me? And what exactly were they expecting me to do? Why did I get the feeling they were all hoping I was some sort of knight in shining armor? I had no armor, and who in heaven's name was I supposed to be rescuing?

Oliver! They were hoping I would rescue the amazing Detective Dawson. But from what? He seemed to be perfectly capable, even with his blindness. I rapped my knuckles on the wooden door and heard Oliver's musical voice ask me to come in. With yet another sigh, I turned the doorknob and entered his small office.

"Yes?" My heart raced inside my chest as I laid eyes on the man who had bewitched me. Oliver was sitting at his desk, the laptop open in front of him, an expression of annoyance on his face. I had interrupted something. "Is that you, Dory?"

"No, it's me." Had the air become thicker? I was having trouble breathing. His lips curved into a smile and I relaxed a little. "Marcy. Can I come in?"

Oliver stood up and waved me to the chair on the other side of the desk. "Marcy, so glad you're here. Sit down." I obliged. "What a nice surprise."

"I understand it's your lunch hour, and I was wondering if you'd like to have lunch with me." Not 100 percent true, but also not a total lie. I smoothed the fake gray tie printed on my shirt, all nerves and jitters. "You don't have to, but it would make me very happy." *So I can swoon over your blue eyes over a sandwich.*

Oliver's well-shaped lips curved into a bigger smile, and I licked mine in automatic response. *I wonder how they taste....* "Nothing would make me happier right now, little witch." The nickname sounded like a beautiful song on his lips. "I'm ready when you are." He punched some keys on his laptop, closed the lid, and stood up, reaching out for the cane resting against the desk. "Dory normally comes and picks me up. She's a sweetheart. We will probably cross ways with her."

I stood up and walked around the desk, avoiding the corners and the inevitable bruises I always got when around tables, to come and hold on to his arm. My hand went under his elbow and I felt him quiver at my touch. Was that good or bad? His aura was clean, so I guessed good. "I actually met Dory on my way here. She knows I'm your escort today." Somehow the word escort tickled my funny bone, and I giggled. "Not *that* kind though."

Oliver looked at me quizzically at first and then chuckled along with me. We left his office arm in arm and were met with dozens of curious eyes and smiles. Either Oliver was a very popular character in the precinct or these people really liked my quirky looks. Feeling strangely self-conscious, I steered him through the main room out the front door and let out a sigh of relief when the cold air hit me straight in the face.

"Something wrong?" The detective seemed acutely aware of my changing mood.

"We got a lot of strange looks on the way out." There was no reason to hide it from him. "I'm used to being stared at, but that was unsettling."

To my surprise, he laughed. "Cops are a protective bunch. Ever since my injury they have been like mother hens watching over me, making sure I have all I need, that I am not depressed… a little overwhelming at times, but they mean well." He let out a loud chuckle. "It's a true miracle that I'm not round like a ball with the sheer quantity of donuts and other baked goods they make me eat every day."

I stared at him, guiltily scanning his fantastic body from head to toe. "You don't look any worse for the wear." I bit my tongue but it was too late; it was out.

"Ms. Spellman! Are you checking me out?" For a blind man, he sure could see a bit too well. My lusty tone must have given me away. I blushed and shoved my polka-dot-rimmed glasses up my nose.

Opting for the truth rather than trying to blunder my way out of an embarrassing situation, I squeezed his elbow tighter. "Well, it's not my fault that you are a fine specimen of the male species. Shame on you! Making us all swoon over you."

His sudden burst of laughter made me stop in my tracks and stare at him dumbly for a few moments. Oliver had stopped too and threw his head back, his deep and hearty laugh melting my insides with the same effectiveness of fire. I joined him.

"And it's not just us girls. This dude just checked you out twice over." I stumbled over the words as I tried to control my laughter with little success. "How do you do it?"

He wiped his eyes with the back of his hand. "I have

nothing to do with it. Good genes, I guess. My father prides himself on being the most handsome lawyer in town."

We had resumed our short walk to the coffee shop. "Your father is a lawyer like your sister?"

"The whole freaking family is into law." Sobered up now, Oliver spoke with a tartness in his voice that belied his usual warm tone. "I'm the only one who decided to go into a different branch of the law. My father was not too happy."

I opened the door to the Coffee Corner and helped him to a free table. "He wanted you to be a lawyer?"

Oliver sat down and placed his cane under his chair carefully. "Hell yes! I did everything in my power to piss him off." The smile on his face was sour. "I refused to attend Harvard even after I was accepted, took my first degree in criminal justice and then decided to go for a second degree in forensic science and technology. Shortly after, I joined the police force and just about killed my father." He laughed dryly. "How ironic would it be if my first case was my own father's demise? Death by disappointment."

I reached across the table to cover his hand with mine. "I'm sure you exaggerate. He must be very proud to have such a fine detective for a son." Stress on *fine*!

He snorted. "You don't know my father, Mr. Oliver Dawson Sr." Wow! They were one of those families. You know, the kind that always named the first son after the patriarch. Traditional and obviously wealthy. So unlike mine.

Sweet young Dory saved the bitterness of the moment by coming to take our order. I watched Oliver, a little worried I had brought up something he much preferred to keep buried, but he seemed to recover from it swiftly and completely. We had a tasty meal of sandwiches and soup along with bubbly conversation. All was well.

"So, Oliver. I was wondering…." *If you'd be mine.* No, no. I needed to take my mind off his sexy body. Oliver leaned forward a bit. "Would you like to go on a picnic with me?"

I was rewarded with an eyebrow lift. "Picnic? May I remind you that it is winter-cold out there?" I laughed, and he smiled. "It doesn't seem like the right time for a picnic."

"I have a secret place… it will be warm there." Larry owed me a favor. It was time I cashed it in.

"Are you a millionaire with plans of whisking me into your private jet and flying me to the Bahamas?" His chin was resting on his interlaced hands.

I giggled, amused. "You never know. Well, is that a yes or a no?"

Oliver tilted his head to one side. "Is it weird that I can feel you smiling? You're smiling now, aren't you?" I was.

"Being a witch, I can see your aura. Just as weird." My heart was dancing. He could feel me smiling. How sweet was that?

"I can't tell when others are smiling. Not even my sister." His voice had gone down an octave. "So how come I can feel yours?"

I had no explanation for that. I also couldn't explain how he could see my red hair, but I knew it in my heart to be a good sign; a sign that we were meant to be together. We had a connection that could not be disputed. "It's magic." My whisper left my lips of its own volition. It felt like magic, the kind I couldn't conjure up with my incantations and potions. The kind that defied explanation and left you breathless. Blind magic.

Oliver sought my hand still resting on top of the table, and gave it a comforting squeeze. "Of course I would love to go on a picnic with you, little witch. To say I didn't believe in magic just a couple weeks ago…." He left it hanging. Did he mean he believed in it now? "But I didn't know you then, did I?"

OLIVER

"Stop that, Oliver." I had checked the knot on my tie at least three times already, and it was apparently beginning to irritate my sister. "The freaking tie is fine. It was fine the other ten thousand times you've checked it."

I was nervous, as I always was whenever facing my parents. They were fierce snobs who could intimidate the most confident person just by their presence. Being their oldest child didn't make me immune to their sense of superiority. I could only take my parents—especially my father—in small doses. Very small.

"I should have had a couple shots of whiskey before coming." I was only half kidding. The temptation to drink whenever I talked to my father was very strong.

We had been standing at their door for the past ten minutes. The first seven minutes or so had been used to give me time to prepare myself mentally to face my sire, and the last two waiting for my parents' maid to open the door. Deep down I was hoping she would never do it, but too soon I heard the subtle creak of a door opening. It was showtime.

"Good evening, Ms. Eva and Mr. Oliver." The heavily accented voice of the older woman who had been my parents' maid for the past ten years had a TV show quality to it. Then again, our family could have very well been imagined by a TV writer. "You father is waiting."

Eva cupped her hand under my elbow and led me through the wide hallway of my childhood home into the living room. I remembered it well and, unlike other children, not in a nostalgic way. I had always hated that house. It was cold, big enough to house a small army, and sterile. The living room where my mother and father received all their guests was a huge monster decorated with the most expensive and ostentatious furniture ever created. Even now in my darkness, I could smell the heavy scent of old musty leather and money. I felt nauseous.

"I was wondering when you'd come." My father's voice reached my ears and my body immediately reacted by shuddering. I couldn't help being immediately transported back to my childhood and teen years, when hearing his voice meant having to do something unpleasant and contrary to my temperament or beliefs. My early years had been filled with his wishes; the horribly stiff and cold private school I went to, the "friends" who were allowed to come over and play—bullies or bores who had nothing in common with me. Even the tiny, uncomfortable suits I had to wear to go to all the formal events to be introduced to more people who only cared about what was in it for them. My girlfriends, all scrutinized and put through the wringer to make sure they were "suitable." I shook my head to dispel such memories.

"The traffic was terrible." Eva was great at making plausible excuses. "We can't stay long, Father. I have a meeting with that client I told you about."

"So good to see you, Oliver." I felt my mother's hand touching mine. Her skin was smooth as usual, her cold fingers making me flinch in spite of myself. "Dinner is ready, son."

I had been quite independent even since becoming blind, but as soon as I was around my parents my senses got mixed up, and I felt like a little boy in a dark room, lost and scared. The scream in my chest was fighting to get out. I pushed it down deeper into myself, trying to suppress the panic being in that house always caused me. *Pull yourself together. You're a grown man.* When my sister let go of my arm after leading me to a chair at the dining table, I almost bolted.

Dinner was served while Eva entertained my parents by telling them details of her last high-profile case. If there was someone rich or famous involved, they were hooked. I sent her a silent thank-you and played with the food on my plate, my appetite mostly gone. Time seemed to stretch in painful slowness. My thoughts went to Marcy, the memory of her crystal-like laughter soothing my nerves and making me smile. I realized with some surprise I had it bad for the little witch. It was a little scary considering my track record, but also heart-thumpingly amazing.

"What are you smiling about?" My father's voice yanked me from my happy place and into the icy hell of his house. "Inappropriate as usual. We're talking about a criminal case and he laughs." I could almost see him looking at my mother, his hand raised in front of him, fingers pointed in my direction in accusation.

I took a deep breath. "I was not laughing, Father." Stupid to argue with a man who considered himself to be right about pretty much everything, from the most banal of arguments to the big bang theory. Yet I couldn't stop myself. I had been defying his views ever since I was old enough to not give in to my fear of him. Since the day I realized I was taller and stronger than my formidable father and I could now stop his heavy hand from beating me.

"Blake came to see me the other day." I'd known he would bring her up. It was stronger than him. "She is still hoping you change your mind, you know."

My hand came slamming down on the table, rattling the dishes and silverware. "I don't want to talk about Blake. This is none of your business, Father." Silence fell in the room. I could hear my father's heavy breathing. He was furious, his face most likely turning red as he came to terms with the fact he couldn't pull out his belt and swing it at me anymore. "Eva, sorry to mess up your dinner, but could you take me home or call me a cab?"

"Don't be a fool, son. You need to listen to reason. Blake is not someone you should just ignore. She's Senator Clover's daughter, for God's sake." And there it was again; the emphasis on status, on wealth and power to the detriment of all else.

I stood up, sending the chair flying across the floor behind me. "Eva? Please." I felt my sister's hand on my elbow, and I followed her away from the table and toward the front door. "Wonderful dinner as usual, Father."

Eva didn't utter a word until we were halfway to my place. I couldn't tell whether she was angry or purely resigned with the fact my father and I couldn't share the same air for more than a few minutes at a time. "Say something, Eva. I'm sorry to ruin your dinner again." The evening was a repeat of another disastrous attempt at a family meal a little over a month ago.

"You didn't ruin anything, Oliver." Her usually steady voice sounded shaken and unsure. "I'm on your side. Father is a jerk, a bully. He hasn't changed. I tolerate him because he is my father, but I don't like him or support him, especially in what pertains to you." She was silent for a few minutes, and then I felt the car turn slightly and stop. I know it was too early to be home so Eva must have parked the car somewhere on the way. "I know what he did to you." My head snapped up. She knew? "I'm not dumb, Oliver. Our house might be huge, but I couldn't miss it if I tried. Burying my head under a pillow didn't stop the screaming, the crying, the yelling... the sound of hard leather against flesh and bone." Was that a sob I heard? "I'm so sorry, Oliver, so sorry."

"It's not your fault." Why was she blaming herself? "You were just a kid like me. I'm glad he never turned on you like he did on me."

"But I could have called the police… I could have done something, but I did nothing. I muffled my crying in the mattress and let it happen. For years." The words, choked by tears, made my heart bleed. The last thing I wanted to do was inflict my pain on her. I was a grown man and my father hadn't laid a hand on me in years. At least not physically.

Reaching out for her, I realized it was the first time my sister and I had a heart-to-heart conversation about my father and his less-than-savory behaviors. "You have nothing to be sorry for, Eva. Nothing at all."

We had never been very affectionate toward each other, so I was shocked when she pulled me to her in a tight hug. "You're my brother and I love you. I may not have been there for you when we were young, but I'm here for you now." And just like that I lost my composure and allowed the tears of the once ten-year-old battered and lonely boy to run freely down my thirty-five-year-old face.

Rain Forests & Hero Sandwiches

The hot, humid air hit us as soon as we crossed the threshold. "Holy shit! You weren't kidding about the heat." Oliver raised his nose up in the air as if trying to place the scent that surrounded us like an unexpected hug. "Are we in a forest of some kind? One that has a door?"

I giggled softly, steering him toward the spot where I had staged our picnic, a checkered blanket spread on the mossy ground and a great big picnic basket brimming with goodies by its side. "We're in the Rain Forest exhibit of the Academy of Sciences." Larry was more than happy to allow me in after hours for my special picnic. "The guy in charge owed me a favor." I had prepared the ointment that had cleared a rather nasty and virulent rash on a part of his body Larry would rather never mention again.

We sat down on the blanket, side by side, our legs touching lightly. "I thought of taking you to the planetarium, but the fact that you wouldn't be able to see any of it kind of put a damper on that plan." Was this a bit too honest? The way he laughed and shook his head put me at ease. "So, I thought where can I take him where his other senses can be wowed? This came to mind." Here he could feel the heat licking at his skin, smell the greenery of the jungle, the musty scent of the wet moss, and hear the animals around us.

"How many guys have you brought here?" His eyebrow curved all the way up.

"You're my first. The others wouldn't enjoy the racket of the insects, the birds, and the occasional roar of the lions."

Oliver laughed. "There are no lions in the rain forest." He had forgone on his usual classic suit and was wearing jeans and a denim shirt instead.

"Okay, the roar of a jaguar then." I pretended to be annoyed. "Mind you, those are recorded sounds. No dangerous animals in the exhibit."

He let out an exaggerated sigh. "Well, that's good to know. I was starting to wonder whether you brought me here planning my demise." As if I would even consider it! Unless his demise consisted of me smothering him with kisses. His face became serious. "Thank you, Marcy. This is lovely."

Anxious to lighten up the mood, I waved my hand in the air, belatedly realizing he couldn't see it. "Thank me again when your clothes are stuck to your body because of the tropical humidity."

Larry had arranged for us to be alone in that part of the building for the remainder of the evening and into the night, as long as we were out of there by midnight. The doors apparently locked automatically from the outside at a certain time, but they could still be opened from the inside. We were all alone, and it felt heavenly. We ate by the light of the sleeping "sun"; talked and laughed without fear of being heard by anyone.

"I love your smile." Oliver tilted his head and then shook it, realizing what he had said. "I'm sorry. I know it sounds ridiculous for a blind man to say that, but I can— It's hard to explain." He looked slightly despondent.

I reached out for his hand and brought it up to my face. "I believe you can feel it. People always mock me when I say things like that, but I know them to be true. You don't need eyes to see." His fingers, long and warm, brushed across my cheeks all the way down to my lips. I shivered.

"I've wanted to do this since the first time I heard your voice. Touch you…." His fingers fanned over my lips in a maddening caress that made me whimper inside. "You're beautiful." His middle finger slipped between my parted lips, and I had to stop myself from taking it in my mouth. Instead, I lifted my hand to his face and mirrored his movements.

Oliver had the most luscious lips I had ever seen on a guy; pale pink, well-defined, and full. Parts of me ignited at the touch. "I've been wondering how they taste." Shit! When would I ever be able to stop my lips from uttering my every thought?

His lip curled slightly at the corner. "Who are *they*?" I hadn't realized, but we had been drawn closer to each other like giant magnets. My face was now mere inches away from his, my leg almost overlapping his as I swiveled to face him.

I couldn't lie. "Your lips. I wonder how they taste." Was that my heart making all that noise?

Oliver smiled and slid his hand behind my neck, his fingers burying themselves in my wild red curls. "Why don't you find out?"

I must have jumped because next thing I knew I had my mouth locked with his. On my knees, I leaned forward and wrapped my arms around his wide shoulders, pulling him closer. His lips welcomed mine with surprising gentleness. I was ready to swallow him whole, while he carefully pried my lips apart and met my tongue with his. Chocolate and coffee! He had the intoxicating flavor of dark chocolate and tangy Arabica coffee, the perfect balance of sweetness and bitterness. I was not much of a coffee drinker, but *this* I could so get used to. Grateful that I had worn my striped shorts instead of a dress, I sat on his lap, straddling him and wiggling closer. I moaned into his mouth as he suckled on my lower lip, tugging on it gently with his teeth. I felt him stretching his crossed legs underneath me, the denim of his jeans rubbing against my bare skin.

"Well?" I didn't hear him at first as I panted over his mouth, stroking across the scratchy stubble on his face and chin.

Reluctantly I moved my face away from his to look him in the eye. The striking blue of his disarming eyes met mine, and I had to remind myself he couldn't really see me.

"Well what?" My voice was husky and raw with the red-hot yearning in my gut.

"How do they taste?" The devil had a wicked smile on his lips. "Worth the try?"

I felt so comfortable on his lap I wondered if we hadn't maybe been lovers in another lifetime. "I'm not sure." I licked the corner of his lips and felt him shiver. *Good.* "I may have to try it again and find out." Oliver forgot about being gentle then and devoured me, his tongue demanding and exciting as it played a game of cat and mouse with mine. Revising my earlier statement, I cursed myself for not wearing a dress instead of the unwelcoming barrier of my shorts. I wanted to feel him wholly, and our clothes were not being cooperative.

Oliver's hands danced their way underneath my T-shirt and up my back, pulling and stretching the fabric until they were flat against my shoulder blades, crushing me against his hard chest. "You feel wonderful, little witch." His mouth traveled around to my ear, whispering voice caressing my skin, lips nibbling my earlobe. I moaned again.

Crazed with the desire for more, I pulled my shirt over my head, exposing the pretty, sexy polka-dot bra I was wearing. *Damn! He can't see it.* The next-best thing would have to do. I sought his hand and led it to one of my breasts. It was his turn to moan. "I wore it for you. Do you like it?" He replied by cupping and kneading my small breast. I threw my head back in pleasure, realizing this was no second best to anything. His hand was playing havoc with my senses and I wanted to do the same to him.

Frantically I pulled on the snaps of his denim shirt until they came undone. Relinquishing his hold on my breast, Oliver shimmied out of the shirt and raised his hands as I yanked his white T-shirt over his head. *Double swoon.* Oliver didn't just look amazing in clothing; he had an upper body to die for. I stared at his chest muscles, his strong but lean biceps, and couldn't stop myself. *Must touch.* Lowering my face to him, I pressed my lips against the base of his throat and made my way down to one of his pecs while my hands held on to his waist as if for dear life.

"I'm sorry, Marcy, but—" The voice stopped midsentence and it took me a few moments to realize it wasn't mine or Oliver's. "Holy shit! I'm so sorry. I didn't know…." Larry was standing just a few feet away from us wearing an expression of utter shock as he took in the full scene; me in my frilly bra, Oliver bare chested and winded. I almost felt sorry for the poor guy, who finally turned his back on us to give us some privacy.

"You told me we could have the space until midnight." I didn't move. It felt safe and comfy—not to mention extremely exciting—to sit on Oliver's lap. The thickness of his jeans could no longer hide his reaction to me, and I was enjoying it fully.

Oliver turned his face toward Larry, his eyes out of focus. "What's going on?"

"My boss hadn't told me that they rented out the place for an event tonight." Larry was still turned away from us, but I could see him biting his nails, a nasty habit. "You guys have to get out of here now so I can have the place ready for the party."

Oliver groaned as I wiggled away from him. "Give us a minute," he said. I looked at my handsome cop and smiled despite my annoyance. "I need a moment to cool off." Sliding my T-shirt over my head, I giggled as Larry choked and coughed at Oliver's request.

We were left by ourselves. Fully dressed now, I offered Oliver my hand. "Grab my hand. I'll help you up."

Once on his feet, he pulled me against him. "This is not over, little witch." No, it wasn't. It certainly wasn't.

OLIVER

"You dog!" Marc was beside himself apparently, and I was beginning to regret having told him about my picnic with Marcy. "You guys met like—yesterday! And you're already all hot and heavy? I'm so fucking jealous right now."

I sighed and dropped my forehead all the way to the top of my desk. If I slammed it just hard enough I may forget about this conversation. "What do you have to be jealous about, Marc? You have a girlfriend. Are you telling me you never have sex with her?"

Marc coughed a little, and I took that to signify he was a bit repentant of his comment. "Well, yes. But I didn't get that close until I knew her for a few months."

"I hate to point this out, but you were in a freaking hospital bed for most of the first few months after you met her." So was I. A bullet in your chest will do that to you.

"Do you think that maybe that's why you guys didn't get it on until much later?" Talking to Marc was often like talking to a child. A child with a lot of muscle and plenty of testosterone.

"I guess…." He sounded hilariously despondent. "But I'm still jealous. Having sex in a rain forest? Holy fuck! And I mean that literally." I couldn't help but laugh along with him. Marc had this infectious laughter that always got me going.

Still choking on laughter, I followed the sound of his chuckling with my eyes. Funny. He also had bright red hair like Marcy, but I couldn't detect it on him. What was that all about? "And we did not have sex, by the way. We got rudely interrupted by the guy who runs the place." Whom I would much like to choke with my bare hands.

"Details… you copped a good feel, didn't you?" That was it! Marc's filter—or lack thereof—needed to be fine-tuned. "Don't give me that look! You did, didn't you?"

"For God's sake, Marc. Can you be any crasser? This is Marcy you're talking about. Not some whore in a bar." I was serious. I had never been much for so-called man talk, but Marcy was definitely out of bounds for this kind of language. "I mean it, Marc. Just be a bit more respectful, please."

There was silence for a moment and I feared I had gone too far, even for my thick-skinned friend. But soon enough he spoke again. "I get it. I'm sorry. You're right. You know me, don't mean it in a bad way but…."

"It's okay." I didn't want him to feel bad for being himself. Especially considering he was a great guy. "Did your mom really teach you to talk like that?"

Marc laughed heartily. "I may have exaggerated a bit the other day. My oldest brother was my tutor in everything obnoxious and culturally offensive." I heard him plop himself on the chair across from my desk. "Are you ready for lunch? I'm starved, dude."

Marc had caught me as I was going over some notes from a cold case, nothing too pressing considering the mystery hadn't been solved in over ten years. "Yes, we can go. Usual spot?"

Dory greeted us at the door, a bit surprised I was early for lunch. She was still coming to get me every day and help guide me to the coffee shop, even though by now I could find my way by myself. It was kind of endearing, and if it made her feel good to help me, then who was I to deny her that pleasure?

We sat at our usual spot, a small square table by the window. I enjoyed the fact I could feel the cold or heat from outside as I leaned my shoulder to the window, and the movement of the cars and people outside always caught the attention of my otherwise inactive retina. It gave me a comforting sense of hope that one day maybe I would see again.

Marc ordered his lunch, a massive hero sandwich with a side of mac and cheese, and Dory guessed what I wanted. I normally got the same, usually the special of the day. The owner of the place was a frustrated chef who liked to offer something different and gourmet-like every day. I found that I liked her choices. The fact that I often ate something I had never eaten before made the drudgery of my life lift for a few fleeting moments and offered me a bit of adventure.

"How serious are you about this girl?" Marc asked, tapping his fingers on the table. I assumed he was talking about Marcy, not Dory.

"It's too early to tell." In all honesty I had already made my decision about her, but even my lust-muddied mind could tell our romance was progressing a bit too quickly for comfort. "I do like her. A lot. She is different from the other girls I dated."

"What girls? Who are you kidding? You haven't dated at all since the shooting." He was right, but that didn't make me feel any better.

"I date… not much, but I have dated a few women." I took a lady friend to dinner a month or so ago, and I may have gone to a concert with another, even though it was not clear if it had actually been a date or a chance encounter. Marcy was indeed the first one I was even remotely interested in. Not because my testosterone had let me down. However, the fact I couldn't literally see the women I met did often have the unexpected—and unwanted—effect of indifference toward them. Not with Marcy. Her voice, the red tinge of her hair in the corners of my darkness, and her scent all conspired to make me hard within seconds of contact. Not a feeling I was used to anymore. In fact, if I was truly being honest, it was not a feeling I had ever been used to. Not to this extent.

Changing the subject seemed to be the safe way to go, so we talked about sports—another thing that had lost some attraction—and work-related issues instead.

"I hear you went to visit your father the other day." Damn it! How did that information leak out? "How did it go, man? Is your father still the same douchebag he was when you were in the hospital?" My father had rubbed everybody the wrong way during my extended stay in the hospital; nurses, doctors, and visitors equally disliked my poor excuse for a parent.

"Yes. He will never change since he thinks he is God's gift to humankind." Father was always right. Even when he was monumentally wrong.

"I still can't believe the arguments he had with the hospital staff about every ridiculous thing." The coffee was too old or too cold. The blankets were scratchy. The television did not have all the news channels available. I was being given too much pain medication, he claimed at some point. I was a Dawson, after all. A Dawson was used to pain and did not require to be constantly sedated. When I argued that I had been shot in the chest and having a hole carved into your skin, muscle, and major organs was not a walk in the park, he called me a weakling, an embarrassment to the family name.

"Well, yeah. I used to think my father was an alien from another planet." It was a joke to distract Marc from this conversation. I had no wish to talk about my cruel and unreasonable father with anyone, not even my best friend. It worked. Marc laughed and went back to the subject of the local hockey team. I sighed in relief.

Marc prattled on and my mind wandered off to sweet

Marcy. I could still feel the heat of her breasts in my hands, the silkiness of her bare skin on mine, the heady scent of lavender and cinnamon in the crook of her neck. The fabric of my pants strained against my reaction to those very vivid memories. Foolishly, I wished I had the power to teleport myself into her arms and finish what we had started the other night. Marcy had done what no one had been able to do before her; she had resuscitated not only my sleeping hormones but also my cold heart. I had no doubts; Marcy was indeed a witch.

Secrets & Insomnia

MARCY

"Are you sure this will work?" Celia was sitting across from me in a booth of our favorite coffee shop, the Old Bookstore, frowning at the agate stone I had just given her. "It's pretty but looks just like any other rock."

"I soaked it in lily of the valley for the past three hours." I could still smell the sweet, flowery scent of the oil on my fingers. "You give it to him and ask him the question. He won't be able to lie to you."

"Marc normally does not lie, but I have a feeling he's just saying yes to please me." Celia was fiercely independent, and the idea that her boyfriend may be going along with her suggestion only to make her happy did not sit well with her. "If going to Paris on our first couple vacation is not his thing, I want to know. I'm sure there is a place we can both agree on."

"Trust me on this. That agate will work." She pocketed

the gemstone and smiled at me. "How's your sis and her hot boyfriend?"

"Up to her eyeballs in wedding preparations." Celia's sister, Emily Rose, had finally settled on a date for her wedding to her childhood friend, Jem. Their whole courtship had been complicated, to say the least. "They are having a very small wedding but she is so picky about stuff."

I laughed, remembering how Em had been so suspicious of my potions and premonitions. When her very ordered world fell into chaos, I had gone to the rescue along with Celia, but she had been very reluctant to accept my help. "Well, tell her that if she needs a calming elixir or something else to let me know. I don't charge my friends."

Celia squinted at me and I knew she was just about to get nosy. "So, Marc tells me you have been visiting the handsome detective at work." Celia's boyfriend was the other cop who had been shot at the same time as Oliver. "Is it getting serious? Come on, Marcy, do tell," she whined, and pouted.

With a shake of the head I gave up. She was my best friend and I didn't keep secrets from her. "I don't know if I'd call it serious, but we kind of got it on the other day." It would have gone much further if Larry hadn't shown up.

Like a teenager, Celia waved her hands in the air and squealed. "Oh my God, Marcy. How was it? Is he as delicious as he looks? Does the eyesight thing get in the way?"

"Take a breath, Celia." She was almost hyperventilating. "To answer your questions, it was amazing. Yes, he is yummy, and no, his blindness is no issue. Happy now?"

She feigned outrage. "Of course I'm not happy. That was an awfully brief summary… how far did you guys go?"

That was too nosy even for me. "I'm not going to give you details, my meddling friend."

"But you always did before." Celia pouted and batted her eyes at me.

"Before was not with Oliver. He's different." There! I said it. It did feel very different with him. Unlike with my other dates, I wanted this one to turn into a real relationship. I wanted to hear the most beautiful three words in English from his mouth. And I wanted to keep it selfishly mine. "Sorry, Celia. I can't explain it, but…."

Celia entwined her two hands together, rested her chin on them, and batted her eyes. "My bestie's in love." She was not mocking me. Celia was possibly the one person in the world that totally understood and loved me for who I was, besides my parents. My mom and dad had been free-spirited people who were taken from this earth way too soon. I had been orphaned right after I had turned fifteen, and spent the next few years in one foster home or another, surviving on the meager tenderness of memories.

I had met Celia in community college quite by accident. She was in the nursing program and I was trying to convince one of the deans to allow me to put a spiritual sciences program together. I wasn't very successful until my best friend-to-be—who had overheard the conversation—came to the rescue. She knew someone on the board of directors who was very interested in metaphysics and the like. She would talk to him about my idea. A few weeks later, she called me and told me the college was opening a certification course in the spiritual arts starting the next semester. We were inseparable after that. She even found the time to audit a couple of classes with me and be my sounding board when I needed to try out new ideas.

I sighed. There was no point in fighting it. I was indeed helplessly in love with Oliver Dawson. Not because he was a hottie—which he certainly was—but because I had felt a connection, a bond that was totally new to me. The kind of connection my parents had had, and I'd always dreamed of having. I was almost twenty-six and, to be honest, pretty lonely. Being unique often was.

"You are, aren't you?" Celia grabbed for my hand on top of the table. I smiled and nodded. She squealed again. "So exciting. Should I start making plans for the wedding?" I slapped her playfully across her upper arm. She was constantly making wedding plans for everyone. I was sure she was driving her sister insane with all her ideas. "I should have been a wedding planner instead of a nurse."

Oliver had called me earlier to tell me he would be stopping by the store later that day. Could I please have more of his tea ready for pickup? He'd sounded very formal, and I figured someone else was listening to the conversation. After my coffee with Celia, I practically ran to Polka Dots and Eye of Newt just down the street, to prepare for his visit.

After some totally unnecessary dusting, lavender dropped in the diffuser, a quick dismissive glance in the mirror to straighten the pink bow on top of my usual eruption of messy curls, and a touch of lip gloss, I was ready. I never wore makeup unless it was Halloween, or the few times I had gone to Mardi Gras in New Orleans with Celia. I had been blessed with thick eyelashes and great skin. I figured I should be grateful and show off what nature had given me.

The chimes rang and I click-clacked my way to the front, my heart racing.

It wasn't Oliver. "May I help you?"

The woman standing a few steps inside the door was tall and elegant. Her very blond hair was tied in a perfect French knot, and her expensive dress hugged all her sensual curves from the neck to her knees. I was beginning to attract the upper classes, it seemed. I smiled at my own thought and stepped forward. "We have a solution for every ailment."

The woman turned her hazel eyes to me and I shivered. How could such a beautiful creature hold so much ice in her stare? She smiled then, but somehow it was even worse. I felt an icy finger run down my spine, and unconsciously hugged myself.

"Are you the witch?" Her rich, sexy voice was as cold as her eyes, reaching my ears as a blast of arctic air. I nodded, my voice frozen in my throat for a moment. "I hear you are very good at what you do." The tone did not match the words, and I knew immediately that she disliked me. A lot.

"Thank you." I prided myself in following the strict rule of *killing with kindness,* and this stranger was not going to make me change that. "Can I help you with anything?" *Like getting you a flying broom so you can get out of my shop.* There was a maleficent vibe coming from her that was making me very uncomfortable. People were inherently good, with a few rare exceptions. This beautiful woman was one of them. Evil seemed to ooze from her eyes, her voice, and her aura. I had only seen another aura as black as this one a long time ago. I had hoped never to see another.

"No. I just wanted to meet you. See you face-to-face." That was a strange thing to say. I wasn't a celebrity or anything. Why would she want to meet me? "I like to know what I'm up against." The conversation was getting even stranger now. "You know what they say; keep your friends close and your enemies even closer." I was neither her friend nor her enemy. Hell, I didn't know her from Adam.

"I'm sorry. I don't quite understand what you are talking about." Might as well ask. "I don't know you, do I?"

Her laughter rose up in the air like poison-filled bubbles that could explode at any time and kill us both. "Goodness, no. We don't move in the same circles. But you are acquainted with someone I know very well. Oliver Dawson."

My heart flip-flopped. How could this horrible woman be in any way connected to my sweet detective? "You know Oliver how?"

She brushed an invisible hair from her face. Rings—expensive ones by the looks of them—adorned every finger, even the thumb. "Well, I'm Blake Dawson." Another sister? I realized I knew almost nothing about Oliver's family. "Oliver's wife."

Through the years I had developed an extraordinary

sense of balance that allowed me, among other things, to walk around in extremely high heels all day long if I chose to—and I often did. But at that moment I almost fell from the tops of my beloved sparkly blue stilettos. What? Had I heard it correctly? "Oliver's wife?" I must have blinked a dozen times in the space of a few seconds. "Oliver is married?"

She put her elegant, long-fingered hand to her mouth. "Oh, I'm so sorry. He didn't tell you?" I could guess a little evil smile lay behind her hand. She was enjoying my distress a little bit too much. "I hope he didn't make you any promises he can't keep."

Oliver had made me no promises, but he also had not mentioned a wife. Quite an important detail to withhold from the woman who had just got half-naked with you. How could my instincts have been so wrong? I was a very good judge of character, and my empathic skills had not given me any reason to think Oliver was tricking me into thinking he was a free man.

Not wanting to give that unpleasant woman a reason to feel victorious in any way, I lied. "Mr. Dawson and I have a professional relationship. Nothing else." My hands were shaking as I hid them in the folds of my pleated skirt.

Again, she laughed as if I had just told her a joke. "You're funny, Marcy. I know about the fantastic tea that has saved my husband from his debilitating hallucinations. However, don't make the mistake of thinking I'm dumb enough to believe your relationship stopped there. You don't have to explain yourself. Now that I've seen you, I'm not worried anymore."

She waved one of her finely manicured hands in the air and spun on her heels to leave. Before she walked through the door, she turned toward me one last time. "Interesting shop you have here. Goodbye."

The door opened and closed, allowing one blast of cold air to sweep through the store and hit me viciously across the face. My eyes stung, but I refused to cry. How could I have been so wrong about Oliver? I must have stood frozen in place for a long while because the light from the sun outside shifted. When the door chimed again, my feet had grown roots and I couldn't move. Oliver, holding on to his sister's arm, walked into the store, sunshine on his back creating a sort of halo around him. I let out a quiet sob and looked at my shoes as if asking them for help.

"Ms. Spellman, good to see you again." Eva moved carefully across to me, a smiling Oliver by her side.

"Marcy." Oliver was still smiling, offering his hand to me. I couldn't take it. I couldn't speak. "Are you all right?" *Damn it!* Why could he feel my moods as well as if he was looking at me?

"I'm fine." I bit my lip and managed to finally move out of the spot I had been grounded to for who knew how long. I led them to the small lounge area and offered them a seat. "What can I do to help you today?" The formality in my voice must have been obvious to him because he frowned.

"Eva, will you give us a minute?" Oliver touched his sister's hand lightly. "I need to talk to Marcy."

"I will be in the Old Bookstore. Give me a call when you're ready to leave." Eva got up and walked away, leaving me all alone with her brother.

I debated how to approach the sensitive and oh-so-very-painful—to me at least—issue of his undisclosed matrimony. Nothing good came to mind, so I just chose total transparency. "Why didn't you tell me you were married?" Oliver, now seated across from me on the love seat, started, his whole body going rigid, followed by a rapid succession of eye blinks. "Didn't it occur to you that I would like to be in possession of such an important bit of info? When I sat on your lap, didn't you think that maybe—just maybe—it would be a good thing to mention your wife?"

"Marcy, I—" I wasn't done.

"I may be a free spirit, quirky and different, but I draw a line when it comes to dating married guys." An unusual and unwelcome anger boiled in my chest, threatening to spill out of me. I was in love for the first time in my whole life, really in love. With someone already taken. "I'm no home-wrecker and I won't be played with by anyone. Not even you."

Oliver took a deep sigh and dropped his hands to his lap. "Let me explain. Please, Marcy…." He lowered his voice to a mere whisper as his jaw muscles twitched and moved under the freshly shaved skin. "Please."

I swallowed the ball of fire that had been making its way up my throat. "I don't know what you can tell me that will make this situation any better. But I'm willing to listen." Listening was one of my superpowers. Not one I wanted to have right now. The power of transmutation would be better about now, so I could change into molten rock or something else that could not feel, could not hurt.

The object of my adoration clenched his jaw again and rubbed his thighs with shaking hands. "I should have mentioned Blake—my wife—but the truth is I just forgot." Forgot? How did you forget your wife? He bit his lip. "We are technically still married, but Blake and I haven't lived together for a long time." Didn't all adulterers say that? He swiped a hand over his hair and then down his face. "It's a long, insidious story, which I will share with you, but for now you must know that we are in the middle of a divorce. Papers are being drawn as we speak and, if it wasn't for the fact that both she and my father are fighting tooth and nail for a cancellation of the divorce procedures, we would have been divorced by now. She has been out of my life for over two years. Ever since I received proof of her indiscretions."

The fireball inside me was slowly fading. *Is he telling me the truth?* "She cheated on you?" Why would anyone married to this amazing man cheat on him?

Oliver nodded, his azure eyes searching for mine—or so it seemed. "Many times over. I suspected for years, but I never knew for sure until a couple years ago when I asked a friend of mine on the Force to find out. It was not my proudest moment—asking a friend to spy on my wife—but I was tired of the suspicion, the bickering, the doubt…. Our marriage was never fantastic, or even my idea in the first place, but I take my commitments seriously." He looked at me then with those unsettling unseeing eyes. "You got to believe me, Marcy, I am a one-woman man. I would never, ever be unfaithful to someone I was promised to. And I would never deceive you."

Words escaped me. I was hurt, the anger simmering away in my gut but still very much there. My heart, on the other hand, was telling me to go to him, wrap my arms around him and tell him it was okay. I sat on my hands.

"That said, it was wrong of me not to tell you about Blake." Oliver rubbed one hand on his neck. "I was so excited to have met you. All these new feelings percolating inside of me… what am I saying? I did not mean to hurt or even hide it from you. I was only too happy to forget about Blake and the living hell she has put me through, and focus on the beautiful silver lining brought on by this condition." He overemphasized the last word, spitting it out as if it was contaminated with something evil. "Focus on you. Since I met you, I sometimes forget I can't see. Because I do see *you*. I see you in all your splendor of colors, sounds, and scents."

I couldn't hold it anymore. Springing forward off the chair, I sat next to him, my arms enveloping him whole. "I'm sorry too. I'm sorry I thought you were deceiving me." My lips touched his ear, a kiss filled with words and feelings. "It's okay. I understand." I did. His aura had turned to a sickly aubergine as he spoke of his estranged wife, reflecting a massive amount of pain and regret. He was not lying about their marriage being over.

"I'm still sorry I didn't tell you and I'm sorry I hurt you, however unintentionally." He pulled me closer to him, his lips mimicking mine, making me quake in pleasure. "You are the best thing that has happened to me in a long time, and I don't want to lose you."

You won't. Not if I can help it.

OLIVER

The horrible smell tickled my nose as I braced myself to gulp the tea down. *It's good for you, fool. Drink it already.* Marcy's tea was a true miracle brew. My hallucinations had dwindled to nothing since I started drinking it, but man did it smell terrible! I chugged it down in one big gulp and squeezed my eyes together in anticipation of the aftertaste. Holy shit, it was bad. I felt for my toothbrush on top of the sink and brushed my teeth and my tongue enthusiastically, trying to get rid of the taste as fast as I could.

I was still shocked at Blake's brazen appearance in Marcy's store. How had she even found out about the little witch? She must still have her spies in the precinct. Not everyone had bought her as the villain in our marriage. There were those who still thought I had been unfair to her. Blake could be very persuasive when she wanted to be. Maybe I should tell Marcy not to visit me at work anymore. For her own safety. My soon to be ex-wife was psychotic and, I wouldn't doubt, dangerous as well.

My head was still spinning when I finally stretched out on my bed that night. Guilt flooded me for neglecting to tell Marcy about my crazy spouse. I had been so busy with the small storm that was Marcy that I had forgotten my previous life. The life I would gladly put away in the dark recesses of my mind, so I could concentrate on making the little witch happy. My hand went to my chest and automatically rubbed the scar left there by that bullet a year ago. The memory of it hurt worse than the wound itself, but I often touched the scar, as if making sure it was healed, making sure I hadn't dreamed the whole thing. I spread my hand over my bare chest and closed my eyes. Before I lost my sight, I used to wonder why blind people closed their eyes to sleep since they couldn't see anyway. Now I knew there was some comfort to be had from knowing the darkness around you was caused by your closed eyelids, not from your eyes themselves.

Blake had always been on the side of unbalanced even in her early twenties. I had met her during a presidential ball in DC. While I tried my hardest to fade into the background, my father fawned shamelessly over my future wife, throwing the two of us together as if we had no will of our own. Even though I was not happy with the situation, my male ego was stroked by the young socialite's interest. Blake was well sought by most males in DC, a great beauty with flawless skin and the sparkling blue eyes of a goddess. She smiled, and men turned into giant puddles of goo, mindless and helpless against her femme fatale charm. As much as I would like to think I was immune to her wiles, I was no different from all the other poor schmucks she had ensnared in her tangled web. So when she revealed her less balanced side I swept it under the carpet of charming quirks and even though I was not—then or ever—in love with her, I was most certainly captivated.

Memories of Blake were never welcome. I tossed onto my other side, burying my face in the pillow and grunting. Hell, I had been young and so stupid I made a dunce look like Einstein. Everything about Blake read *danger,* and yet I had somehow managed to ignore the signs and swallowed the bait, hook and all. In the process I had made my father proud for the first time in my life. Ironic, really. I had to tie a metaphorical noose around my neck in order to impress him. It didn't last long, of course. In less than a year my wife revealed herself as the psycho she truly was, and it was a downhill road from there. When I'd told my parents I was considering a divorce, my father had reverted to being the always-and-forever disappointed father. A father who was more than willing to sacrifice the happiness of his own son in order to keep a family connection that served his hunger for power. It had been five long years of fighting and mostly losing battles to put some distance between me and my wife.

With all the tossing and turning, it became obvious I was not going to get any sleep tonight. My audio books would have to keep me company for the next few hours and work their magic to erase all the bad memories exploding in my head.

Old Friends & Makeout Sessions

MARCY

"You're making me nauseous." Celia pointed her fingers at her mouth and made a gaging sound. Em, still glued to Jem's lips, waved a dismissive hand at her. "Get a room or something."

"I think they're cute." They were. As a firsthand witness to their romance and misadventures a year ago, I thought the fact that they were now together and engaged to be married soon was totally adorable and romantic.

"Ugh. If Jem sticks his tongue any deeper in her throat we will see a sudden reappearance of her breakfast." Celia was always finding ways to nag and bother her sister and future brother-in-law. It was a weird—and yet endearing— facet of their relationship. "You don't want to see that, right, Marc? I know I don't."

Marc sat next to us in the café booth, an amused smile on his lips. He was a lean mountain of muscle topped with an eruption of even brighter hair than mine. The skin on his face was lost beneath a thick layer of freckles, and from between his red, pale lashes a pair of clear blue eyes sparkled like diamonds. "Aww, let them slobber all over each other. They've been through so much."

Celia huffed and puffed until she realized that neither the couple in question nor Marc and I were going to side with her in this matter. Shrugging and letting out a loud sigh, she leaned back into her boyfriend's chest. "I just don't get it. They've known each other their entire life. How aren't they tired of each other?"

"Are you saying that after we date for a while you'll get fed up with me and go on to someone else?" Marc winked at me and I covered a giggle with my hand. "Well, good to know that your love is really that flimsy and shallow."

Not one to get intimidated easily, Celia smacked him playfully across the chest. "Don't make me mad or I will show what I'm capable of." The smile on her face belied the threat in her words. Marc wrapped his arms around her and pulled her into a hug. "You're crushing me!" He laughed out loud, hugging her even closer.

As happy as I was that both Celia and her sister had found the loves of their lives, I always felt a little empty, a little left out. Love had not been a constant—or even a variable—in my life. Now that my heart had given in to Oliver Dawson's skillful wiles, I still felt that tinge of jealousy that always made me feel guilty and unworthy of such good friends. The fact that Oliver was still married also rankled big-time. I had never pictured myself as a home-wrecker and had no intention of starting now, no matter how much I craved the tall, handsome detective. I wanted to believe him, I wanted to accept that he had indeed been separated from the ruthless Blake for a long time now, but doubt still gnawed at the edges of my conscience.

"Marc, you and Oliver are friends, right?" Why not just come out and ask someone who knew the truth?

The red-haired cop let go of Celia and smiled at me. "Yes, we have worked quite a few cases together. He's a great cop and an even better guy."

Something had been bothering me ever since I had discovered he was one of the cops shot while on protection detail for Em and Jem. "If he is a detective, why was he assigned to guard our friends here? Isn't that unusual?"

The kissing couple had finally come up for air. "Oliver, the other cop that was shot with you?" All that kissing had distracted them from the earlier conversation we were having. "You're dating that cop?"

I felt the tips of my ears burn. "I'm not dating him." *Liar, liar your ears are on fire.* "He's a customer."

Marc laughed, and when I gave him the look of death he tried to cover it by pretending he was coughing. "He went on a few of those assignments with me. By his own request."

I pushed my pink-rimmed glasses up the bridge of my nose. "Why? Why would a detective request such a thing? Doesn't that normally require to be away from home for a while?"

Wrapping a solid, thick arm over Celia's chest, Marc shook his head. "That's exactly why he did it. He wanted to have some time away from his crazy wife."

My heart sputtered like an old motorcycle. "Were they still living together?"

"God no! Dawson kicked the bitch out almost two years ago, but she is relentless." Marc had his fingers entangled in Celia's necklace as he spoke. "Every time he thought the divorce was about to be final, she would come up with some detail, some loophole to drag it out longer. She had the help of his father, who absolutely adores his daughter-in-law and can't accept that the marriage is over."

My muscles relaxed and my heart went back to its normal rhythm. "Then why try to stay away if they weren't living together anymore?"

"Because his psycho wife was constantly dropping by, calling, even sneaking in the house and waiting for him to come home from work to ambush him in bed." Marc's emotional tone confirmed his friendship with my love interest. "One day he came to work with a black eye and a stab wound in his hand. He claimed he had got into a fight with some hoodlums in a bar the night before, but I knew him better. Oliver was never the barhopping kind and he would never, ever get into a fight. He's too levelheaded for that."

I leaned forward. "Are you saying Blake did it?" Was it even possible? Was she that psychotic?

"Hell yeah, she did it." Celia twisted her neck a bit to look at her boyfriend's face. His face had turned a bright hue of pink. "He never confirmed it, but I know she did it. He would never lift a finger against her but she most definitely would, pissed off enough."

"Why won't she give him a divorce? Wasn't she cheating on him anyway?" Celia was suddenly interested in the conversation. She loved a good drama. Jem and Em had also leaned forward, listening.

"Because she wants the family money and the status that comes with being Oliver Dawson's wife."

I shook my head, not quite comprehending. "Oliver is a cop. He can't make that much money, can he?"

Marc laughed. "No, that he can't. I can attest to that. But he is from some serious family money and his whole family is well connected in DC. Status means a lot to Blake."

"But the divorce is going to go through soon, right?" It was Emily Rose, her face twisted into a concerned grimace. She looked at me for confirmation.

"Yes, the papers are now being drawn finally." Marc planted a light kiss on Celia's cheek. "They should be ready to be signed within the month."

I felt the massive amount of air that had collected in my lungs release. That was so good to know. Even better to find out Oliver had been telling me the truth. "Good! Because I do not date married guys."

Em jumped forward, her finger pointed at me. "Ah! I knew it! You *are* dating him." She put so much emphasis on her words, we all burst out laughing.

Jem stood up and came to put his long arms around me. "Little Marcy, I hope this is your chance at love. It couldn't happen to a better person." Then he whispered for my ears only, "I won't ever be able to thank you enough for helping me and Emily Rose."

After they left, I sat by myself, cradling my teacup and lost in thought. So much so, I didn't realize someone had slid into the opposite seat. "Why aren't you smiling?" Oliver, in an impeccable blue suit and holding a simmering cup of fragrant coffee, sat directly in front of me. His gorgeous blue eyes seemed trained on me even though I knew that was impossible.

"What are you doing here?" I scanned the café, looking for whoever had brought him here. "How did you get here?"

Oliver smiled. "My sister brought me but she had an appointment, so she left right away. Do you want me to leave?"

I actually cackled like an old hag. "Of course not. I'm glad you're here." Without thinking I sought out his hand over the table. "I was thinking about you."

"With or without clothes?" A silly rise and fall of his eyebrows made me laugh again.

"I was thinking about how much I enjoy your company."

"And you're not mad at me for not telling you about Blake?" His voice dropped to a whisper as he held on to my hand.

Without hesitation, I squeezed his hand and said, "No, I think I understand why you didn't mention her."

"Thank you, little witch. I had trouble sleeping last night, thinking I may have involuntarily pushed you away." His astonishing eyes softened. "I would never forgive myself if I did."

"Well, you can relax." I meant it. I was totally over it.

"You're smiling, aren't you?" It was truly uncanny how

he could tell. I gave his hand another squeeze. "You know, you have the most beautiful smile in the world."

"Flatterer." The widening of my smile contradicted my accusation. I loved that he could tell when I smiled. Boy, was I in way over my head, crushing on this beautiful man! Hard to believe that Marcy, the witch, was in love for the first time.

We sat quietly for a while, holding each other's hands. There was so much I wanted to ask him, so much I wanted to say. But for now this silent moment was enough.

OLIVER

The lights flickering caught my attention. I could see the rapid flashes of light to my left as the smell of burning candles wafted all the way to my nose. Marcy's soft voice reached my ears as a caress. "Terra, Ignis, Aqua, all three elements of astral, I summon thee earth by divinity, divinity by earth give thy enemy the power to see."

I smiled. The little witch was casting some kind of spell. Shortly after I'd arrived at the store one of her customers had come in with a request for a protection spell. Marcy hesitated to leave me alone, but I assured her I would be fine in her small lounge area while she did the voodoo that she so beautifully did. "I don't do any voodoo!" Her outrage had made me laugh. "That is dark magic and I'm a white witch."

"Sorry, Marcy." I reached out to her and touched her

face, a small gesture of appeasement and apology. "I was just quoting the song." Her face leaned against my hand and I knew she wasn't mad.

"I'll be quick. A protection spell is a pretty simple one and it takes only a few minutes." I could now hear her chanting the incantation from the kitchen area. "The strength of the elements by my side, rules of magic, I shall abide." It was strange, even a little bizarre, but music to my ears. If someone told me a few months ago that I would be dating a witch, I would have laughed. Look at me now, smitten like a teenager with their first crush.

My father had been calling me daily, the phone's ring and vibration running through me as if he was physically there, screaming at me. I was not going to answer, of course, but the very idea he was calling me made me anxious and angry. What did he want now? To convince me not to divorce Blake? To make me feel like the worst son in the history of the world? To drive the it's-your-fault-it-didn't-work nail into my insecurities coffin? Throughout the years I had gotten better at ignoring the stabbing insecurity his judgments inflicted on me, the searing doubt he was always able to stir up in my heart. But I was not totally immune to it yet. Not by a long shot. He was my father, and it didn't matter how cruel, how unfair I knew him to be, his sharp and poisonous opinion of me would always find its mark.

"Make sure you carry the amulet at all times." Marcy's voice snapped me out of my bad thoughts and I instinctively turned my eyes toward her voice. Strange how I still did that even though I couldn't see. The doctors claimed that was a good sign. That it meant I may one day recover my sight. I personally thought they were just saying what they thought I needed to hear to carry on. There was a kernel of hope inside me, but I had come to terms with the very real possibility of being blind for the rest of my life.

The chimes of the front door sang and I knew the customer had left. "Are we alone now?" Marcy giggled and the sound of her stiletto heels made their way toward me. "Is it okay to kiss you to an inch of your life now?"

"I dare you not to." The little witch sat down on my lap and I was hard instantly. Damn! How did she do that? Her lips met mine, and I stopped thinking. The scent of lavender took over my senses, relaxing but heady all at the same time. She tasted of cinnamon and oranges as her tongue made its way between my lips and met mine. "You don't seem very serious about your threat," she taunted.

On fire, I swept her off my lap for just a moment, leaned her down on the sofa and covered her with my body. "Is this better?" Our kiss became frenzied, urgent as if we couldn't get enough of each other's taste. In the back of my mind— way in the back—I wondered how I was going to explain the wrinkled suit when I went back to work. Who cared? All my body and I could think of was my sweet little witch and how her skin would feel under my touch.

"Fuck! You should put a warning sign at the door." Marc's voice yanked us out of our make-out session as effectively as a pair of strong hands. I sat up, a little dazed and seriously annoyed with my best friend. "Good thing your friend is a few steps behind me." The door chime rang again. "Hey there,

Celia, you just missed…." He trailed off as he registered my warning grimace.

"Celia, Marc, what are you guys doing here?" Marcy had sat up as well. Her hand lay lightly on my hip, reminding me of my uncomfortable state of arousal. I shifted on my seat, hoping to God my pants were not revealing what I was feeling.

"Came to take you guys to lunch, of course." Celia plopped herself between Marcy and me. "Marc knew Oliver had come to see you, so here we are." Her voice changed from perky to hesitant. "You are happy to see me, right?"

"Of course I am." I felt the couch shift ever so slightly as they both stood up. "Come and help me clean up in the kitchen, and then we can go."

"Sorry for interrupting the make-out session to end all." Marc sat down next to me, laughing softly. "Dude, you guys were going at it. With the front door unlocked. Ballsy."

"Shut up, Marc." I wasn't really angry at him. It was a good thing he'd come in when he did. As much as I craved the little witch's body, there was something terribly wrong about the idea of making love to her in a public place. She deserved so much more than a quickie in the lounge area of Polka Dots & Eye of Newt. I was going to woo her in grand style. I had quickly become aware that Marcy meant a lot more than just a roll in the hay for me. I was not sure yet what that *more* meant, but I knew that the first time we made love was going to have to be special. My little witch deserved nothing less.

Cottages & Sleepless Nights

"I'm blind, but even I can tell you drive like a madwoman."

I giggled. Oliver held on to the door like a drowning man to a piece of driftwood as I zoomed through the rush hour traffic heading out of town.

"For a cop, you are certainly a serious chicken." I squawked a couple times for emphasis. I had picked him up at the end of the day from the precinct for a weekend escapade. I thought—and Oliver agreed—that there was much we needed to talk about before we could move on with whatever was developing between us. I was pretty new to the concept of a real relationship, so I was winging it, so to speak.

"You're going to love this place. Providing, of course, that you don't kill us first." I swerved to avoid a misguided squirrel and nearly hit a car coming the opposite way. I cringed silently and hoped Oliver wouldn't realize his prophecy had almost come to pass. Oliver had reserved two rooms in this bed-and-breakfast in a quaint and sleepy little town just an hour away from home. As usual, I had overpacked, filling the whole trunk with two suitcases and several bags full of stuff I was sure I would never have the chance or the time to use. Oliver's overnight and garment bag had been thrown rather unceremoniously on the back seat of my Beetle as he made himself comfortable in the passenger side.

"How did you find out about this place?" I had visited Edenburg a couple times, mostly to shop in the many vintage and antique stores that made their home there. But I had never stayed overnight. Like most of this type of towns, rooms—even in bed-and-breakfasts—came at too much of a dear price for the owner of a not-so-busy witchcraft store.

The town lay at the bottom of a mountain range, well sought-after by both hikers and skiers. Despite their beauty, mountains had always scared me for some strange, unknown reason. This time was no exception. As we approached town and the mountain suddenly loomed on the horizon, high and mighty, thin tendrils of fear began wrapping themselves around my throat. The sense of danger was so strong I could not only feel it; I could smell it and hear it humming in my ears. I shook my head to dispel such thoughts. I was going to spend a whole weekend alone with the man who had so quickly claimed my heart. What was there to be afraid of?

I realized that Oliver was talking while I was distracted by these unsettling thoughts, and I tried to bring my focus back to his voice. "My parents used to own a house here and we would come for weekend breaks all the time." I noticed, not for the first time, the catch in his voice when he mentioned his parents. "They sold the house many years ago and, as far as I know, never came back. Not trendy enough for them anymore."

He fell silent and stared ahead. Stealing a glance at him, I noticed that this was the first time he actually looked blind, his eyes motionless, unblinking and unfocused. *What are you thinking?* He hadn't had a chance to change before we left, so he was still wearing the expensive-looking charcoal two-piece suit he had worn for work. Oliver had unbuttoned the jacket and loosened the knot on his tie, which now ran over the white shirt like a narrow maroon stream. Butterflies invaded my stomach. Suddenly, images of his bare chest popped in my head and left me breathless. I gulped and made myself focus on the road ahead.

To get to the bed-and-breakfast I had to drive through the small town and up the mountain a few miles. The smaller building where the two rooms Oliver had rented were located was set apart from the main building of the inn, half-hidden in the thick forest. The sun had set, and snowflakes had begun floating down from the skies, reflecting the lights illuminating both buildings. Oliver had called the owner as soon as we arrived at the outskirts of town and, true to his word, the man waited for us by the carriage house.

"Mr. Dawson. It's a pleasure seeing you again." The man rushed to the car to help with the luggage and seemed slightly daunted by the quantity of bags in my trunk. "You're only staying the weekend, right?"

"Yes. I have a tendency to overpack." The man relaxed visibly. "I have trouble deciding what to bring with me." Oliver giggled and tightened his hold on my arm as we strolled to the building, several bags in tow. "This is beautiful, Mr…?"

"Call me Joe. Mr. Dawson and I have known each other for a long time." Then why was he still calling him Mr. Dawson? "Let me get the door for you."

The dark wood structure had an aura of otherworldly beauty in the shimmer of the outdoor lanterns and dusted by the falling light snow. We stepped into a cozy living room area where a couple armchairs and a sofa piled high with colorful cushions faced a large, flaming fireplace. The walls stretched up to the high ceiling, past the balcony where the bedrooms were. I spied a small kitchen and a breakfast nook under the railing and right of the narrow staircase leading upstairs. A sense of comfort and peace descended on me, dispelling the earlier uneasiness. This was a good place.

Joe returned from his trip upstairs with a few of the suitcases to find me still standing in the hallway, studying my surroundings and holding on to Oliver's arm. "I hope everything is to your liking, miss."

Oliver looked down at me and smiled. "I think she likes it." How did he know that if he couldn't see the stupid smile on my face? "She's smiling."

The owner looked at Oliver, his eyes wide, and then back at me. I smiled at him. "Don't ask me how he can tell, but he can."

After a brief explanation of where to find things and

other housekeeping instructions, Joe left us. We had the whole building to ourselves, Oliver told me. Even though there were four rooms in the carriage house, he had reserved all of them so we could have privacy and not deal with the curiosity of others. "I didn't want to hear people wondering how the blind man snatched such a beautiful girl."

I laughed, dropping my blue, flowery coat on the nearest chair. "Yes, they wouldn't be able to understand how a good-looking guy could ever attract anyone." I spun on my heels to take a better look around. "This is beautiful, Oliver. Great idea."

Oliver stripped off his jacket after pulling out his retractable cane from his pocket. "The best thing about this place is that I have been here often enough since the surgery to be able to navigate the space on my own." As if to demonstrate his familiarity with the place, Oliver walked around the massive coffee table to the sofa. My mouth fell open. How did he do that? Did he have some kind of bat-like sonar sense? He laughed as if sensing my surprise. "I have asked the owner to put everything in the exact same place it was when I was here the last time. He told me he had marked every spot with special tape, so he wouldn't make a mistake."

"You must have paid a fortune for this place." I couldn't imagine having the kind of money that went into reserving a whole building like this for a day, much less for the weekend.

"One of the perks of being rich." It was stated simply but stained with a certain sourness.

He didn't elaborate, so I had to ask. *Curse my mouth!*

"Since when are detectives rich?" I sat next to him on the sofa, admiring the comfort of the mismatched seats.

"When his family is filthy rich." Definitely sour. "Sorry. Didn't mean to snap at you. My family wealth is sometimes a bone of contention with me."

I touched his hand. "But it has its benefits sometimes, right?" I giggled to let him know I was joking. I felt him relax under my touch, and a smile lit up his face. "Shall we go check the rooms in this joint?"

Oliver laughed. "You go. I have seen them many times. Well, so to speak…." I hopped off the couch and ran up the stairs, feeling like a young girl getting ready to check under the Christmas tree. I was not disappointed. The rooms were small and exuded the type of comfort I felt at home with. I inhaled the warm air as if it was perfume, and I felt my lungs inflate with a promise. My spell was active and working.

I changed into my pajamas, a cloudy heaven of cottony softness, and I heard Oliver climbing the stairs and closing the door to the room next to mine. I went downstairs and settled myself on the couch, legs curled under me, and enjoyed the warmth of the roaring fire. Through the window I could see snow falling, heavier than before but not enough to cover anything yet.

The man who came down the stairs later was someone I barely recognized. Used to seeing Oliver in suits, I was not prepared for the relaxed, at-home version that came to join me on the sofa. He was wearing a pair of thin, soft cotton pajama pants that hung low on his hips, and a slightly darker blue henley shirt that stuck to his muscles like a second skin.

Heat rose from my gut all the way to my face and I had to fan myself with a cushion.

"Are you hot?" Oliver asked, a cocky smile on his lips. Mr. Hotness knew!

"Not used to being so close to the fire." I could play that game. Besides, I was not even lying. I wasn't used to being so close to the kind of fire he stirred up in me. "What are we eating?" Belatedly, I realized we had not brought any food with us.

"I arranged for a small dinner to be delivered to us in a few minutes."

"Well, aren't you Mr. Suave with all the right moves." He shrugged and lifted his hands up in the air in a not-so-sincere apology. "I feel like a queen today."

"I haven't even got to the royal treatment yet." The veiled promise in his deep voice caused another wave of heat to flow straight to my cheeks. A knock on the door saved me from making a fool out of myself.

The "small" dinner turned out to be a three-course meal that we ate on the small nook table after Oliver threatened to make a huge mess of himself if he had to eat on the couch. The soup was hot and soothing, the main dish—a delicious concoction of sole and rice—was like a party for my taste buds, and dessert…. "I can't eat anymore." I was so full, the simple act of looking at the gorgeous créme brulée in front of me made me nauseous. "I'm saving this for later."

After dinner we sat on the rug by the fireplace, our backs supported by the sofa, my short legs crossed, his long ones stretched in front of him. I watched him, slightly guilty he couldn't see me doing it. His hands were lying beside him on the rug and I instinctively touched one. He smiled.

"I want to see you." The statement was as surprising as endearing. "I know I can't physically see you, but I can see you inside my head."

I drew small circles on top of his big hand, feeling tiny electric shocks caress my whole body. "And how exactly do you intend to accomplish that?"

His luscious lips stretched further and his eyes shone in the twilight. "You be my eyes." *Uh?* "You describe yourself to me."

I cringed. "I am not very good at talking about myself."

"That's one of the things that makes you so beautiful." He was so good at saying the right thing to mollify me. "But do it for the poor blind guy who wants to know what the girl he's dating looks like."

In spite of my unease, I had to laugh. "Okay. I'll do it." He whooped. "But only because you *are* a poor blind guy."

Oliver wiggled as if adjusting his position for better listening. "I'm all ears."

I swallowed a ball of anxiety and searched for the right words. "I'm pretty short—"

Oliver interrupted me. "I know that. Probably about five two?" I nodded, ignoring the fact he couldn't see me. "I want real descriptions; colors and feelings. Your own rain forest."

I groaned. "My own rain forest indeed." I sighed and fell silent for a few seconds. "You know my hair is red and curly. What you may not realize is that I have a head full of messy, frizzy curls that refuse to be tamed. That's why I normally wear my hair up in a bun or a loose braid like tonight." Turning around to face him, I brought his hand, still in mine, up to my hair, lying to one side of my face. "I like bows. A lot! Some say a bit too much. Celia often says I look like a birthday gift begging to be opened." He opened his mouth to say something. "Don't say it! Don't even think it." But *I* was thinking about him unwrapping me with those hands of his and…. I shook my head. "You're distracting me."

"In a good way, right?" His hand playing with my hair was definitely distracting.

I ignored him. Kind of. "I wear big, funky glasses because I am waiting to win the lottery to have corrective surgery. But I do like my glasses a lot."

"They add to your personality," he suggested helpfully.

His hand had slid to my cheek. I automatically leaned into it. "My skin is your typical redhead skin; alabaster with a spatter of freckles across my nose and cheekbones—not many, which is surprising for a red like me." The heat of his palm spread from my cheek to my neck and parts beyond. He had scooted up to me and his body was now so close I could feel his heat. "I have a tiny nose—not very handy for glasses—and my eyes take over my face; round and big like smoky blue marbles."

"And your lips?" Oliver's voice was low and husky, thick with undisguised desire. His fingers skirted the contours of my lips, taking my breath away.

"I have been blessed—or cursed—with naturally red lips."

My voice caught in my throat as his fingers touched the corner of my mouth. "You know the rest…."

"Not well enough yet." He leaned over to me and I met him halfway.

Our mouths fit together like two pieces of a puzzle, his tongue teasing my lips apart and caressing mine. My insides burst into flames, and so did my face and my ears. I moaned into his mouth and he replied in kind as his hands slid over and around my shoulders to cradle the back of my head. I felt his fingers play with the rubber band of my braid, coaxing it out until my hair fell free of its constraints.

Oliver pulled away from me slightly and began pulling my braid apart, my wild curls flying every which way around my face. "This is why I never wear it down." I was surprised I could still talk. Oliver's kiss seemed to have some strange power over my usually high-functioning vocal chords. "It flies all over my face."

His amazing blue eyes looked straight into my soul as he grasped some of my curls in his hand and brought them to his nose. "You smell like sunshine and flowers." The lava inside of me bubbled up and melted everything in its way. Still holding my hair, he buried his lips on my neck behind my ear, and flickered his tongue on my skin. I may have squealed in delight. "I do want to know the rest of you, all of you."

I was game if he was. I had never been very inhibited when it came to sex, but with Oliver it would have to be more than that. So much more. I needed a deeper connection with him. One that spanned beyond the physical into our very souls. But my body was burning with desire, and I was more than willing to take that step. Much to my surprise, Oliver stopped me when I began trying to peel off his shirt.

"Not yet." His breathing was ragged, and I bit my lip to prevent myself from kissing him again. "There is much we don't know about each other, Marcy. As much as I want this, it's too early." A little confused that a guy actually wanted to put the brakes on a possibly epic make-out session, I remained silent for a moment. Oliver sought me out with his hands, touching my lips as if assessing my mood. "You're not mad at me, are you? You're not just another girl. You're...."

I shushed him with my mouth. Mad? Of course not. The fact that he wanted to go slow with me made him that much more endearing and sexy. When we separated, our lips hovering over each other's, breathing harder than if we had just finished a marathon, I was tempted to make him change his mind. "I love that you want to get to know me first," I said instead. *A bit hypocritical, no?* When all my girly parts were screaming in protest. "So what do we do now? I'm afraid to move." I was. I was scared that if I moved, even an inch, I was going to throw myself at him again.

Oliver dropped his hands from my hair and scooted back just enough to create a chasm between us. I sighed mournfully and dropped on my butt and against the chair behind me.

"Not fair, to get me all hot and bothered and then step away." I pouted and crossed my arms against my breasts, which were aching in frustration. Oliver chuckled. "You are wicked, did anybody ever tell you that? All sexy and with freakishly strong self-control. Not fair at all."

Oliver jumped to his feet with a grace that belied his large stature. "Little witch, I think I'm going upstairs to take a very cold shower now." He felt on the floor beside him for his cane, and headed for the stairs. "Good night, Marcy, and thank you."

"For what? Unfinished business?" I was still pouting like a child.

He laughed again. "No, not for that." His face settled into an expression of sheer happiness and I couldn't help smiling. He was as beautiful inside as he was on the outside. "Thank you, little witch, for coming into my life."

OLIVER

What was wrong with me? I mean, really. How could I, a red-blooded male, have stopped that amazing red-haired witch from making love to me? What the hell was wrong with my brain? The blindness seemed to have brought something even more insidious along with it. Something that was stealing my inherent instincts as a member of the male sex.

Not totally true, though. I had been on fire from head to toes downstairs, and still was as I lay in bed tossing and turning like a dog seeking the perfect spot to claim as my own. I wasn't even sure how I made it up the stairs and into the very cold shower. The flames of unadulterated lust had scorched my whole body.

With Blake and others that came after, I had often jumped in bed with them on the first date. In the words of my filter-deprived friend, I wanted to get laid, pure and simple. It was more complicated with Marcy. Sex was very much on my mind—and in every pore and cell of my body—but there was something else. Something I had never felt for anyone, scary and exciting. I couldn't put a name to it yet, but it was definitely putting a damper on my sex life.

I heard the little witch come upstairs and stop by my door. My heart cartwheeled. Was she going to come in? I wanted her to, with every fiber of my body. A mixture of disappointment and relief washed over me as I heard her walk away and close the door to her room. Realizing I was holding my breath, I exhaled deep and long. Hell, she didn't even have to say or do anything to turn me hard as a stone.

My book was on my nightstand. I adjusted the headphones to my ears and pushed the play button. Maybe a good mystery would distract me from the red-haired enchantress sleeping next door.

After an hour of listening to the same paragraph over and over again, I gave up on any pretense. My skin was alive with feeling, as if covered in a layer of electricity. My witch would not leave my thoughts. I pulled the bedcovers away and swung my legs over the side of the bed, but as I was trying to stand up, it hit me. A shapeless blob of an eggplant-colored creature came at me, and even though the rational part of my mind told me it was an illusion, the rest of it told me to be very afraid. I whimpered and crawled back into bed, closing my eyes but unable to shut the horrifying dysmorphic object out. I had forgotten to drink my tea, and now Marcy was going to witness a part of me I never wanted her to see.

Ghosts & Bad Ideas

I seemed to have grown coils in my body, because no matter what position I got myself in, I would almost immediately bounce over to another. Toss and turn, turn and toss for hours. Or what seemed like hours. I was not paying much attention to the blinking alarm clock on my nightstand. However, I was acutely aware of every little sound coming from next door. The very thought that that thin wall was all that separated Oliver from me made me itchy and hot, as if assailed by some weird strain of chickenpox.

With a giant, loud sigh I flopped myself on my back, eyes wide open and staring at the bland ceiling above me. I couldn't even remember the last time I had stayed awake because of a guy. Yet, here I was, my skin all tingling in frustration, all thoughts of sleep gone by the wayside. I listened—something I had done a million times already— for something, anything that would give me a clue as to how that man next door slept. Did he sleep on his side, a leg crossed over the other, one hand under the pillow? Or was he a back sleeper, mouth open and legs spread apart across the whole width of the bed? I knew he didn't snore. My catlike ears would have caught even the slightest sign of that. But he did toss around a lot. I could hear the telltale subtle groaning of the wooden bed every time he turned. Either he was a restless sleeper or I was also rattling his sleep.

I couldn't be sure how long I lay there, but eventually I must have drifted off to sleep. A muffled sound woke me up. My brain, blurred by sleep, took some time to process what I was hearing. *Oliver!* Propelled by one of those aforementioned springs, I jumped out of bed and ran next door, fueled by the sound of what I could identify now as screaming. The door to Oliver's room was not locked and I barreled through it without much thought about privacy or decorum. The light of a small lamp infused the room in a soft, sleepy glow that allowed me to see inside. Oliver was sitting up in bed, an expression of utter horror in his wide-open eyes. A guttural scream left his lips as I entered, and for a second I thought I had scared him somehow.

"Oliver, what's going on?" I approached the bed slowly at first, afraid of scaring him further, but I could tell I was not the reason for his distress. His blind eyes were focused on something ahead of him, something awful by the looks of him. He was having a hallucination. Now that I thought about it, I hadn't seen him take any of the tea all day.

Running to his side, I sat on the edge of the bed and

tried to hold him, but he swatted me away. With gusto. His arm slapped me across the chest and I lost my balance and fell on the floor. Well, I was not one to give up easy. I may be small in stature but I had the inner strength of Hercules. I got to my feet and this time I crawled on top of the bed until I was next to him. Using my arms like a lasso, I drew him to me and held him there with all my strength while he fought me.

Even though I couldn't say what he was seeing in his mind, I knew it to be horrible. This strong man, who did not allow blindness to control him, seemed helpless against this perceived horror. Moaning and groaning, he tried to shove me out of the way but I had a tight hold on him. "Oliver, it's me, Marcy. Calm down. It's just me."

Time stopped—or so it seemed. I wasn't sure how long I held him there, my face resting on his shoulder as I braced myself against his jerky moves. My arms were beginning to hurt, so I guessed I had been at it for a while. Just as I thought I couldn't hold it any longer, Oliver began relaxing under my hold. Gradually I felt each of his muscles letting go until he slumped over himself, his head resting against my chest. A thick layer of perspiration covered his face as I brushed my hand across it. I cooed as if cradling a child, my lips against his temple. For a moment I thought he had fallen asleep, but then I felt his hand go around me and latch on to my waist.

"You're smiling, aren't you?" I almost laughed out loud as he chuckled softly against me. We both fell silent. "I'm sorry, Marcy."

I let go, sitting next to him instead, propped up by pillows. "You didn't take your tea today." It was not an accusation. He nodded. "I will go brew you some."

As I moved to go he held my arm. "No, not yet. Stay with me for a while." I relaxed against the pillows and I felt his body do the same. He leaned his head against the headboard and laughed quietly. "What a joke. I bring the lovely witch to this beautiful B and B, trying to impress her with my sophistication and finesse, and what do I do? I show her what I look like when my demons come to haunt me. You must be impressed."

Turning slightly toward him, I cupped his cheek and brought my lips to his. "Nothing sexier than to see a man's vulnerable side." My lips barely touched his and yet they burned with the promise. His lips curved into a wide smile right under mine. "But you still need that tea." I jumped out of bed before he could stop me again. "When I come back we'll talk."

Anxious to go back to his side, I rushed through the process of boiling the water to brew the tea I had packed with my other just-in-case herbs. After hurriedly pressing the off button on the timer, I collected a teacup and all the other accoutrements needed on a small tray, and climbed up to his room. He was still sitting up against the pillows but I knew immediately he had tidied himself up. His sweat-soaked henley top had been replaced by a simple black T-shirt, and he had even brushed his disheveled hair.

I laughed. "The vanity of men." I brought him a steaming cup of tea, still giggling under my breath. He held it and gingerly took a sip. "You know I thought you looked really hot with the sweaty clothes."

He choked on the tea. "I sure felt hot, but not in a good way." We both laughed. "I didn't want to scare you with my manly smell."

"You mentioned that your parents used to own a house around here." I was too curious about him. The truth was I knew very little about his life other than what others had told me. "But how come you still come over here often?" *What if he tells me this is where he used to come for romantic interludes with his wife?* But no. He had said something about coming here since he became blind. "Any sentimental attachments to this place?"

"I always loved it when my parents brought my sister and me here. It was the only time we felt like a real family." He laid the teacup down on his lap still half-full. "We used to go hiking in the mountains, and I loved the feeling of the cold, thin air in my lungs and my face, the sense of freedom being alone with nature." He was quiet for a second, lost in thought. "But then my parents sold the place and I never came up here again. Until I got married."

My heart shrank. He did bring his horribly beautiful wife here. Suddenly I wanted him to shut up, or for me to dissolve into the air and materialize somewhere far away. But alas, my witchy skills didn't stretch that far.

"I brought Blake to the mountains once thinking that maybe if I shared my special place with her, some kind of bond would magically form between us." He had a wistful, faraway tone. "Of course, that was both foolish and childish of me. She hated every minute of it, and by the time we left a bigger wedge had been driven between us."

Breathing became a bit easier. "Not a good marriage?" Stupid question. He had already told me that. I had to ask again anyway.

"Seriously? Do you want to hear the whole insidious story of my marriage to the beautiful Blake Clover?" His voice cracked with bitterness.

I nodded and held on to his hand. "Of course I do. Good or bad it's part of your life, and I want to know you wholly."

He gave my hand a squeeze. "I can think of a few much more pleasurable ways of getting to know me."

I laughed and tugged on his hand, urging him to tell me the story of his failed marriage. "Let's go over the unpleasant stuff first."

His lower lip caught between his teeth, Oliver took a deep breath before embarking on his story. "I met Blake in DC a lifetime ago. I was still in college and my father had great ambitions for his only son. My grandfather and uncle were big names in the capital, and my father had hoped I'd either go into politics or become a hotshot lawyer for the powerful like he was. He dragged me to one of DC's galas and introduced me to the much-coveted Blake Clover, daughter of a powerful senator. The family was bankrupt, but still held major connections in the political arena. My father saw an opportunity and wouldn't let go."

"Are you telling me it was an arranged marriage?" I laid my head on his shoulder, relishing his body heat.

"No, not really. It was my decision to marry her, but I

can't honestly say I did not have a lot of *encouragement* to do so." His voice caught over the word, that sour tone making a swift return. "We dated off and on for a couple years after we met. Blake can be very charming when it serves her purpose, and I know now that marrying me was on the top of her goals list. You see, her father had lost the family money in every casino from the metro area up to the west coast. Blake had grown up used to the best and was having trouble holding a job and making ends meet. She also liked the idea of the status of being married to the son of every freaking politician's lawyer. It meant running in the right circles, attending all the right events, and meeting all the right people. Imagine her surprise when she found out she got very little of that once we were married. I had no intention of staying anywhere near DC or moving in the same circles as my father."

I raised my face to look at him. In the dim light of the room, his blue eyes seemed to shine with a light of their own. "If you knew that, why did you marry her in the end?"

"I didn't know that. Suspected some of it, yes, but we were both young and I thought she was just naive and starry-eyed. I thought that once we were married we would both settle into reality, and be happy we did." He chuckled under his breath. "I was so stupid. I'm not sure I ever truly loved her. I was in awe of her. This gorgeous creature whom every man in town wanted to bed wanted me. Me! The prodigal disappointing son of an aging lawyer. A cop wannabe with too much money and not enough sense. I was blinded by her neon lights." He laughed at his own pun. "I can see better now that I am literally blind than when I first asked her to marry me."

I shifted, restless and yearning to put my arms around him and make him forget he had ever met Blake. "When did you bring her here?"

He turned his eyes to me in that disconcerting way of his. "I never brought her here to this B and B." His mouth fell open and worry clouded his eyes. "You didn't think that I...? Oh my God, I would never bring you to the same place I brought that bitch. I don't even go there myself. It was a little, rustic hotel up in the pass. I don't even think it's open anymore." His hands were now holding on to mine as if to assure me he hadn't come to this place as a walk down memory lane.

"Then why this place? You obviously have been here more than once." I allowed him to pull me closer to him, our sides glued together and legs half entangled over the sheets.

"I love the mountains, and even my wife couldn't ruin that love for me." He planted a kiss on the top of my head and I melted just a little. "I wanted to come back and make new memories. I found this place a few weeks before my surgery through somebody at work who had his wedding reception here. I fell in love, and after I was blind, the owners were so accommodating I started coming here as often as I could. Do you like it?"

My hand rested on his chest and I could feel the beat of his heart against my palm. It was like a song that filled me with yearning and joy. "I love it, Oliver. I'm glad this place holds no memories of Blake for you. You came here alone?"

A deep sigh lifted my hand. "Yes. Eva drove me here and then left me for a few days. I needed the time alone." He hesitated. "The truth is, little witch, I was depressed. I have accepted it now and rolled with the punches, so to speak, but after my injury I went through some very dark times."

My mind went back to the time of his shooting. Jem and Em had been hiding in the small cottage in the woods with Marc and Oliver as their guards. I had seen it in a vision that morning, the danger coming. Celia was the only one who believed me, as was often the case, and had tried to warn them but it was too late. Both cops had been caught by surprise, shot and left for dead while my friends had been captured and taken by the criminals. It had been a tough few days for all of us. For a short while we'd thought we may never see our friends alive again.

"When I lost my sight I shut down." Oliver coughed, stumbling over his words. "I didn't want to live anymore. My days were spent sitting on a couch in silence, only standing to go to the bathroom. Eva got me a babysitter of sorts, a very nice nurse who I'm sure I put through the wringer with my bad attitude and lack of motivation."

"Whose idea was it to come here?"

"Eva. She had heard me rave about this place before and she thought that it wouldn't hurt for me to spend a few days breathing the good, however rarefied air of the mountains." He sighed again. "The nurse came with me, but she was given instructions to only help me when I absolutely needed it. It was brutal at first, but soon I started exploring the room, counting steps and feeling my way to the kitchen and back, the bathroom… a few days later I had almost mastered my mind map of the place and my depression had shrunk to a manageable size. After that, I came almost every weekend. Something about it just gave me the will to go on in spite of the obstacles."

"I feel very special." Yes, I felt blessed by the fact he was sharing this very special place with me. "Thank you for bringing me here."

Oliver bent down slightly and took my lower lip gently between his teeth. "I can't think of anyone else I would rather share it with." He swallowed me, and I willingly drowned in his kiss. The slow burning I had in my core all night, just erupted into full flame. Turning around, I straddled him and kissed him again, riding the wave of desire running through me. I felt him swell under the thin sheets and I moaned. He wanted me as much as I wanted him.

A loud, strident, siren-like noise stopped my mouth halfway down toward Oliver's lips. We both perked up our heads like cats hearing an unidentified sound. "What the hell is that?" It was too soft to be a fire alarm. "Did you leave something on in the kitchen?" Oliver shifted uncomfortably under me.

"Oh hell! The freaking kitchen timer. I must have accidentally reset it instead of turning it off." *Because I couldn't wait to be by your side.* Reluctantly I climbed off Oliver and walked to the door. "I will be back in a second."

I heard Oliver groan in frustration or annoyance before I sprinted down the stairs to turn the blasted thing off. On my way I tripped over two bags I had stupidly left lying around the living room, stepped on a sugar cube I must have dropped on my way up, and managed to almost fall over one of the small end tables in my rush to the kitchen. Cursing under my breath, I finally made it to the kitchen, took a minute to make sure I pressed the off button this time and not the reset, and then rushed upstairs where a very hot, very attentive Oliver awaited. Or at least that's what I thought.

As I stepped through the open door of his room, I took one look at the bed and knew that there would be no loving that night. Oliver, still propped against the pillows, had fallen asleep, his head bent backward, lips slightly open, and the thin fabric of his skintight T-shirt rising and falling rhythmically with his breathing. I was disappointed. My less-behaved body parts were crushed. But I couldn't be mad at him. He looked so peaceful in his sleep. After watching him fight his demons not even an hour before, his face contorted in pain and fear, seeing him like this now was a special sort of heaven.

I stood there for a few minutes, quietly watching him sleep, my heart beating to the rhythm of his peaceful breathing. Had my spell worked backward? Had I unintentionally made myself fall in love with this man? For someone who had lived all her life without feeling or being the recipient of true love, it was hard to understand how this could have happened. And how quickly it had come to pass. Maybe I had unconsciously reversed the spell, and instead of Oliver falling hard for me, I was the one doing all the falling. It looked like Mother Earth and all her minions had a very strange sense of humor.

OLIVER

My head swirled with the realization of what I was feeling. Holy shit! I was in love. In. Love. Two words I had never uttered to myself much less out loud. It wasn't as if I didn't believe in love. I did. I'd just never felt it myself. I may have tricked myself into thinking I was a little in love with my wife at first, but deep down I knew it was only overwhelming lust. There was no mistaking it this time; I was irreversibly head over fucking heels in love with Marcy, the witch. I wasn't going to lie, it scared the hell out of me.

After my brush with yet another one of my humiliating hallucinations, the weekend had gone from bad to wonderful. I couldn't even remember when I'd last had such a good time simply talking and lounging around for hours. Even though I was disappointed to have fallen asleep when Marcy seemed so willing to make love to me, I couldn't help but being grateful for the time we had getting to know each other better. We walked together in the growing cold of the woods surrounding the carriage house and shared a couple meals in my favorite restaurant in town. We may not have known each other for very long, but after our weekend together I felt as if I had known Marcy all my life.

"Are you even listening to me, Oliver?" My sister's voice was exasperated. I had yet again zoned her out. Marcy was in my every thought, every second of the day. It turned out being in love was exhausting. "Where do you go? You get this blissful expression on your face. Are the angels whispering in your ear?"

I snickered, hiding it behind my hand. "In a way, I suppose they are. Well, one angel at least." A bright-red-haired one. "I'm sorry. What were you saying?"

In an unusual gesture, my sister covered my hand with hers as if to grab my attention. "Dad wants to see you again."

"No way!" I shook my head for emphasis. "I'm not putting myself through that again."

"He promised Mom he would not bring anything up." It was obvious even my sister didn't believe it possible. "Just a short social meeting. In a public place. Neutral." The choppy sentences coming from someone who prided herself on eloquence was extremely telling of her faith in my father's promise. "He starts something, you can just get up and go."

Why was I actually considering it? A sucker for punishment, I was not. In the back of my mind the idea of accepting the invitation and showing I was not afraid of him any longer was a very attractive one.

"I'll be there with you," Eva said, her voice merely a whisper now.

"No, thanks, Eva, but I will take Marcy with me." That took me by surprise. I was going to take poor, innocent Marcy to meet the monster? What was I thinking?

"Marcy?" Apparently I had also taken my sister by surprise. "They'll eat her up. She is so not the kind of girl you want to introduce to our parents."

I bristled at her words. "Marcy is an amazing woman."

"I'm sure she is, but she's also quirky, too colorful for the snobbish eye of our parents…." She paused. "Too outside the norms. Mom and Dad want perfection, or at least what *they* consider perfection. Marcy is a witch, for God's sakes."

Like a petulant child I crossed my arms in front of me. "She *is* perfect in every way."

"You're just trying to goad Father." I flinched. It was a bit too close to the truth. "It's not fair for Marcy. They will judge her with every look. You won't see it, but Marcy will. And you know very well how much those looks can hurt."

Eva was right. I was trying to provoke my father, to go against what he believed in and what he approved of. I was ashamed of myself for even thinking of using the little witch as bait. Yet, the temptation to dig a knife—however small and insignificant—into my father's ego was too strong. I was going to take Marcy with me.

"Marcy will be all right with it." I hoped. "We will be okay." End of discussion.

Bad Blood & Good Loving

MARCY

"I need to go wash my hands." It was the third time I'd required a thorough handwashing in the last twenty minutes.

Oliver took hold of one of my allegedly dirty hands and pulled me closer. "Stop fidgeting so much. I promise they have been fed already today."

"But what if I look like a juicy, tasty cut of steak to them?" I stomped on my high-heeled boots, fighting the instinct to flee.

"My parents are not going to eat you alive." Oliver leaned down and kissed my cheek close to my ear. "No matter how delicious you look."

"Like you can tell." I had tried to look normal-ish. I had put on a mauve shirtdress sprinkled with yellow and pink flowers, a yellow geometric-design scarf, and plain, brown high-legged boots. At the last minute I had added a navy blue sweater and leggings with mini white polka-dots. The dots made me feel safer.

"I sure can." Oliver chuckled. "You smell amazing, and whatever you got on, it's soft and gentle on the skin. Can't wait to remove it all later tonight." Wicked man! After our weekend together in the mountains I had teased him incessantly over the fact he would rather sleep than make mad, passionate love to me. Now, he was paying me back in kind.

"Right. You may not like the chewed-up and spat-out version of me." We were both sitting in a booth of a high-end restaurant in town I would have never even dared go into, much less dine in. Everything looked fancy and expensive, from the pretty, deceptively simple white-covered tables to the tuxedo-wearing waiters who navigated between patrons and chairs with the expertise and speed of race car drivers.

Oliver's parents were to meet us there, and I was a nervous wreck. Nothing I had heard about them led me to believe they would be accepting of me. They sought out people of their own social status, people who exuded elegance and beauty—however superficial—with last names that meant something to the powers-that-be in town and beyond. I was none of those things. Marcy, the witch, was a foster child with no special fortune, family connection, or life-learned elegance and sophistication. I was a wild creature with a taste for loud fashion and whose only gift was that of being able to walk on extremely high heels. I was so out of my league in that restaurant, I might as well be a green, tentacled alien.

"They're not coming. We've been sitting here for half

an hour and they haven't shown up. Let's go home." I must have jinxed it, because I heard the hostess utter their names as soon as I had finished speaking.

"Here they come, Marcy." Oliver squeezed my hand under the table. "Just be wonderful you and everything will be all right."

The *wonderful me* didn't feel that confident. I watched a middle-aged couple be led almost reverently to our table. I could see the family resemblance. Oliver Dawson Sr. was a handsome man, his hair just spattered with silver on the edges and eyes as blue as his son's. Next to his tall and elegantly dressed body was a woman of such beauty my eyes watered from the glare. Oliver's mother was tall like Eva, and while her daughter was incredibly beautiful, Mrs. Dawson's beauty was the kind you see in art museums, ageless and ethereal. She wore a blue ombre dress that hugged her still youthful curves, and a pair of high-heeled black shoes. From her ears, two long showers of sparkling stones I would bet my life were not cubic zirconia fell all the way down to her perfect shoulders. Like a work of art, she seemed out of place, as if she should be encased in some kind of protective glass somewhere safe.

Oliver stood up and I followed his lead. "Oliver." His father's voice was low and well modulated, the voice of a politician. He shook hands with his son in an oddly formal gesture. "Who's the… lady?" I noticed his slight hesitation and my stomach plummeted to join the rest of my digestive organs in a self-pitying feast.

Oliver frowned and held on to my arm. "This beautiful

lady is Marcy Spellman." He may have been preaching calm earlier, but I could tell by the subtle quake of his voice that he was nervous as well. "Marcy, this is my mother and father." No "mom and dad." I ached for Oliver.

The older Dawson stretched out his hand and I shook it. A bit too enthusiastically, I think. Then his mother turned to me and took my hand gently in hers in a loose shake. "Ms. Spellman. A pleasure, I'm sure." I wasn't so sure myself.

"Please call me Marcy, Mrs. Dawson." I foolishly expected her to give me her first name as well, but I was sorely disappointed.

We all sat down around the circular table, Oliver and I on the booth-like padded bench and the parental units—they were too perfect to be human—on chairs across from us. Big mistake. The chairs sat higher than the booth, which meant they both looked down on us through the whole meal—literally and figuratively.

After we had ordered our appetizers—which looked too pretty to eat—Oliver and I sat quietly, hands entwined under the shelter of the linen tablecloth, waiting for the older Dawsons to start a conversation. I thought it odd that Oliver, a thirty-five-year old man, would wait meekly for his parents, but I was the odd woman out and I was not about to give my opinion.

"Marcy, my daughter tells me you have greatly improved Oliver's quality of life by helping him get rid of his hallucinations." Mrs. Dawson lowered her voice at the end of the sentence and quickly scanned the room around her for onlookers. There were none, but for once I was grateful of Oliver's blindness. There was no shame in having hallucinations caused by a brain malfunction. It was not like her son had gone totally bonkers. "How did you manage that? Are you in the medical field?"

Despite knowing Oliver couldn't see me, I glared at him. He had not told his parents about my unconventional profession. "I am not. I'm an herbologist. All I did was to put together some herbs that reduced his propensity for hallucinations." I hated myself for not telling them what I really was, and I hated them for making me feel embarrassed about who I was for the first time in my adult life.

"Marcy is a witch." It was Oliver, clear voiced and loud enough for everyone in the immediate vicinity to hear. I was not sure whether I wanted to kiss or kill him. His parents' eyes opened wide. "She owns a store downtown."

Oliver Dawson Sr. cleared his throat and wiped the corner of his mouth with the immaculate white napkin. "A witch? You mean Wicca?" His steady voice was a little shaky this time.

"Not Wicca. I don't follow their religion. Just a plain white witch." My voice had shrunk to a whisper, not wanting to embarrass them any more than I had to. "Mostly I make teas and potions to help all kinds of ailments."

Oliver's mom was not listening. She had turned to her son and spoke in an oddly loud voice for such undertones. "You went to a witch?" It was more of an accusation than a question, and I slid further into the booth bench.

"Marcy helped save the couple I was protecting when I got shot." Oliver spoke quietly, but I couldn't help hearing the chiding tone underneath it. "If it wasn't for one of her potions, they would have died. I think that qualifies her as someone who knows what she's doing, wouldn't you say?"

"What would Blake say about this?" His father's eyes were shooting daggers, which thankfully Oliver couldn't see.

"What do I care about what Blake thinks? We're getting a divorce, Father. You better get used to the idea that our marriage is very dead and cold. She's out of my life and I'm not letting her back in." I could feel Oliver's hand shake over mine.

"I wish you could be more sensible, son." The older man avoided my eyes.

"I am being very sensible." Oliver's protest came out so loudly, patrons at other tables turned their heads toward us. "Furthermore, Father, Marcy is more than just a friend. We are dating." The announcement surprised me almost as much as it obviously shocked his parents. Mrs. Dawson's pretty face lost all signs of color, and his dad's lips contorted into an angry frown. "I was hoping that for once you would put my happiness and welfare ahead of status, but it seems I was wrong. Again." His hand gripped mine even tighter. "Marcy makes me happier than I have been for many years. It's sad that you can't see that."

Without any more words, Oliver stood up and pulled me behind him from the booth seat. His hand sought my arm. I knew he would need me to guide him out of the restaurant, but I wanted to make it look like he was the one guiding me, so I wrapped my arm around his waist and subtly coaxed him to move in the direction of the door. "Pretend you know where you're going," I whispered.

Oliver walked confidently in the direction I was urging him, but as soon as we were outside he dropped his arms in defeat. "I'm so sorry, Marcy. I don't know what made me think they would be happy for me and accept you for who you are." He leaned back on the frigid wall, clouds of frozen breath spiraling between us. "My father still thinks I will reunite with Blake for the sake of the Dawson good name. They live in a fantasy world that does not include me."

"I'm sorry too, Oliver. I wish I could be more… standard, normal." Hard to believe those words were coming out of my own mouth, but I so wanted to be part of Oliver's world. And being accepted by his parents would make him happy.

His arms encircled me and my body slumped against his. "Don't ever apologize for who you are, little witch. Never." His body heat seeped through my clothes and warmed my shivering heart.

"You don't know what I look like, Oliver. I'm quirky—which is only a nice way of saying weird. You may not feel the same if you could actually see me." *Whoa, where is this coming from?* Was I really scared that Oliver may change his mind about me if he could see me? I realized with a jolt that yes, deep inside I was scared he would also think I wasn't worthy of him. Him, so classical, so clean-cut. Me, strange and unorthodox.

Oliver buried his lips in my curls, now flying free of the bun I had painstakingly tied on the top of my head. "I know exactly what you look like, little witch. You're beautiful and unique, inside and out. Don't you ever change for anyone. Not even for me."

In spite of the freezing cold, I felt warm and comfortable in Oliver's arms. I wanted to stay within their shelter forever. Imagine that! Marcy wanting to be protected and sheltered. I laughed into his shirt and felt him shiver. "You're shivering. Are you cold?" In our rush out of the restaurant, he had left his overcoat behind. He now stood out in freezing temperatures in only his suit jacket.

Oliver's voice thickened. "I am shivering, but not because I'm cold." It was my turn to shake from head to toe as a frisson of pleasure went through me. "Do you want to come to my place?"

I couldn't speak so I nodded like a fool. There was nothing I wanted more at that moment than to go home with him. We had been seeing each other now for a few weeks and we were yet to make love. Hell! We had spent a weekend together alone and even then we missed our chance. It was as if the universe was teasing us, waving the proverbial carrot in front of our noses only to yank it away over and over again. I wanted this man. My sleep hadn't been the peaceful time it used to be before I met him. Instead of relaxing into my usual dream-free slumber, I spent the night fighting with my pillow and sheets.

Tingling in anticipation, and neglecting to collect our coats inside, I drove us to his house on the outskirts of town, a surprisingly small studio apartment on the second floor of an old building. Oliver told me he had sold his old penthouse and bought this tiny place because it was easier for him to navigate blind. There was not much furniture for him to trip over; a simple, frameless bed against one wall, a sofa against the opposite wall bookended by two end tables, a small bistro table and two chairs in the nook by the one-counter kitchen. Simple, uncluttered, and yet so Oliver.

We had just closed the front door when Oliver took me in his arms and nestled me between him and the wall behind me. "I've been dying to do this for a very long time." His breath caressed the side of my neck as his lips traveled to my earlobe. "You smell amazing, little witch." *It's the lavender, not me.* Who cared? I swooned.

Oliver's hands fumbled with the buttons on my dress just as I pulled his jacket off him, sliding my hands between it and his shirt. I could feel his hard muscles beneath it, tensing up and relaxing under my touch. The fire in my belly roared and I was suddenly desperate to feel his skin against mine. With shaky but determined fingers, I unbuttoned his shirt and glided my hands along his ribs and back. Oliver moaned and helped me strip him of the intrusive items of clothing. "I think I need help with these freaking buttons." Still fumbling with my dress, Oliver found my lips and swallowed me whole as if starved for my flavor. I met his tongue with my own in a dizzying dance. He tasted of coffee and promises. "I need to feel you, Marcy. Please."

I pulled apart for a moment, watching him, his breath labored and his eyes burning with desire as I got rid of my belt, sweater, leggings, and dress as fast as I could. "Shit! Too many layers." Oliver laughed softly and I joined him as I threw my dress across the room.

In my underwear, I took a few moments to watch him closely. Shirtless, Oliver was magnificent and blissfully unaware of it, his chest rising and falling rhythmically with his quickened breath. I reached out and brushed a hand over his chest, my fingers tingling against the soft, light cover of dark hair phasing out into the waist of his pants. I closed my fingers around his buckle and pulled him toward me, his bare chest crushed against mine.

"Can I?" The request sounded incongruous considering I was standing half-naked before him, but I loved that he asked. I held his hand and led it to one of my breasts. He cupped it and rubbed his thumb over the thin, silky material of my bra, making me whimper with pleasure. His mouth followed his hand, his tongue playing havoc with my senses. I arched against his mouth and slid my hand to his back and inside his pants.

Oliver followed the track of my bra with his hands to unhook it in the back and throw it over his head. With his hands back on my now naked breasts, I turned my attention to the fly of his pants. I wanted to see him naked, to feel his body against mine, to meet his hardness with my softness… if this was what madness felt like, I was very willing to lose my mind.

Soon enough we were both naked as the day we were born and too intoxicated with each other to stop. Not that we wanted to. We stumbled together all the way to the bed. Oliver fell backwards into the soft mattress, and I stood quietly drinking him in. "What are you doing?" Oliver seemed a little confused and vulnerable lying bare on that bed, gloriously aroused but unable to see me watching him. I felt guilty.

"Just admiring you." I crawled over and straddled him, throbbing with yearning. I moaned as I felt his heat meeting mine. "Oliver, you're so beautiful."

Oliver grunted and I felt him swell further against me. "I wish I could see you, little witch." His hands cupped my breasts and I liquefied inside. Slowly, I rocked against him, working myself up to a peak of feverish longing. "Condom."

Half-aware of his words, I replied with grunt of frustration. I didn't want to stop. I wiggled on top of him, trying against all reason to get closer.

"Marcy, the condom is in the nightstand drawer." In the recesses of my mind, the part that was still able to think clearly, I wondered why he had condoms and whom he had invited into his bed often enough to be prepared for it. Reluctantly lifting myself from his lap, I stretched to open the drawer and collect a foiled-wrapped condom, which I frantically opened, almost dropping it. I was so busy with the job at hand, I almost missed Oliver's whisper. "I love you, little witch."

Naked, aroused, and holding a prophylactic in my hand, I was suddenly assailed by a bout of guilt. "There is something I have to tell you."

The gorgeous man beneath me grunted in frustration. "Traditionally you would say 'I love you' back. Strange time for a confession." His hands slid up my thighs to rest flat on my bottom.

"I have cast a love spell on you." I was not sure what

kind of a reaction I would get, but his laughter was not it. My body shook as Oliver broke up, his lower body arching against mine in a strange mixture of sexiness and awkwardness. "What's so funny?"

"Little witch, you didn't have to put a spell on me. I loved you the minute I heard your voice that first time." I melted again. "Yes, it was magic, but not of your doing. I love you, Marcy."

I love you too. I bent down until my lips met the warm skin of his chest. The words wouldn't leave my mouth, but I could show him how much I loved him. I followed the track of his hard muscles with my lips, down to his navel, unable to get enough of his taste. I fumbled with the condom, anxious to have him inside me. Oliver laughed after I had twice dropped it on his belly. "Having trouble down there, little witch?"

I slapped him playfully and crowned my success with a hoot. "No trouble, Officer. I'm about to make you mine. This is your last chance to change your mind."

"Never." Oliver grasped my waist with both hands, lifted me up, and brought me down again gently, burying himself within me. I threw my head back in pleasure and heard him moan. We were one. I was in heaven. Finally!

OLIVER

Her breath, gentle and at peace, lulled me to a state of semislumber. The little witch was mine, or at least as mine as a human being can ever be. I was most definitely hers, body and soul. Feeling her warm skin against me as she lay by my side, one leg crossed over mine, her knee resting against my hip and her fingers splayed over my scar, I felt at home. Her red hair was spread out next to my face, the one thing in this world I could see. I raised my hand and played with it, swirling it around my fingers, satin against the coarseness of my calloused hands.

A stirring told me she was waking up. "Are you okay?" Her sleepy voice caressed me, along with her hand, which slid down my chest onto my belly. I felt myself respond to her touch.

"I'm fine." Did I slur my speech? That overwhelming feeling I always got every time I was with Marcy took over me again. I turned on my side and kissed her, my mouth fitting over hers like a piece of a puzzle, lips coaxing hers open to let me in. "I'm better than fine." There was no way she couldn't tell how *fine* I was feeling at that moment as our naked bodies intertwined. She giggled softly over my lips and I kissed her harder, my tongue exploring deeper and more passionately. I wanted her. Now.

I rolled her onto her back and began exploring her body with my lips and my hands, tracking my way from the crook of her deliciously warm neck, down between her breasts, lower to the softness of her belly, and lower still. I lifted her legs and rested them on my shoulders so I could nestle between them and taste her. Marcy arched and pressed against my mouth and I moaned against her softness, her heat. I was not going to last very long at this rate.

Hands pulled me away. "Condom." Her whisper made me laugh. She was not going to last long either. I felt my way into the bedside table drawer and wasted no time with subtlety. I handed it to Marcy and lifted myself on my arms to make space for her to roll it on me. The touch of her fingers almost undid me right then. "Behave, Officer. Your time will come." The little minx was messing with me. I realized with a start she had slid beneath me and followed her hands with her lips. To use the cliché, I nearly exploded as her lips closed around me, my arms trembling under my weight.

"I'm not going to last long, little witch." I thought it was only fair to warn her, but she had other ideas. Before I could lose it, she flipped me over and lowered herself on me, her heat throbbing against mine. My hands reached out to caress her breasts and she whimpered in pleasure. I moved beneath her, hips thrusting forward as I drove myself deeper. "God, I love you, Marcy. I love you."

Waves of pleasure held me hostage, but I couldn't help noticing—however far back in the recesses of my awareness—the little witch had not said it back.

Insecurities & Fear

MARCY

"I've made the worst mistake of my life." My words, muffled by the sleeve of my sweater, burnt in my throat. The thought that I could be right made me quiver uncontrollably.

Celia placed her hand on the back of my neck in a comforting gesture. "Don't say that. I'm sure there is a perfectly good reason for it." She had come over to the store as soon as she got my near-hysterical call an hour before.

I raised my mascara-stained face to her. "Oh really? What kind of explanation can you think of?" Celia drew a blank, her mouth half-open as if she was trying to utter some words of wisdom, but none came out. "I messed up. Normally I wouldn't care one way or another. But this is Oliver we are talking about." I grabbed her hand in mine. "I'm in love with him, Celia. For the first time in my life I'm in love. And I go and mess it all up."

My best friend, a worried look clouding her eyes, sat

next to me on the couch. "Honey, you didn't mess up. You just followed your heart. If he is that shallow that he just wanted to have sex with you and flee, then he's not worthy of your tears."

Celia was missing the point. I was not afraid Oliver had used me for sex. Instead, I was afraid he thought I had used *him*. Oliver hadn't called or come to see me all day. We had that epic lovemaking night, and then we met the next day for coffee. We sat at the Old Bookstore and talked for a couple of hours. I was still reeling from his love confession, not sure what to make of it. I wanted to believe him, but the foster child in me found it hard sometimes to fully trust anyone, and I had held back. Now I was afraid that maybe he had misunderstood my reluctance to tell him how I felt about him—other than physically—and had decided I wasn't worth his time. Oliver had seemed a little distracted the day we met for coffee, but maybe he'd already been trying to decide whether to invest in a woman who couldn't even say *I love you* back to him in the throes of passion.

"Have you called his cell?" Celia handed me a box of tissues. "Maybe he has been too busy or something happened. He *is* a cop, you know."

The truth was, I was terrified of calling him and confirming my fears. I blew my nose loudly in a wad of tissues and pulled out my phone. "You're right. I better just get this over." For the last two days I'd had this dark cloud following me everywhere I went. Thick, black tendrils of fear that threatened to strangle me. For the first time in memory I couldn't make heads or tails out of it. What was that aura of fear all about? Normally my premonitions were clear enough that I could make sense out of them, but maybe because my mind was clouded by the feelings in my heart, this time all was fuzzy and unintelligible.

When my call went straight to voice mail I decided to call his work. I punched in the number for the precinct that Oliver had given me, and someone answered almost immediately. I recognized the female officer that usually manned the front desk. "This is Ms. Spellman. Is Detective Dawson in by any chance?"

There was some commotion going on in the background and I heard someone curse out loud. "Sorry, Ms. Spellman. One of our customers is misbehaving." She stressed the word with a tone of sarcasm. "Dawson hasn't been to work in two days. His sister thought he was with you." My heart stopped for a moment.

"He's not home?" The black cloud was taking a more definite shape now.

"His sister says he isn't. He called in to take the day off to take care of something. In fact, that was right before he went to meet with you." The officer paused for a moment as if thinking. "I remember it clearly because we all teased him about it. When he called that evening we all assumed he was going on some escapade with you. He is obviously totally smitten." This comment should have made me feel good, but instead it made me worry even more. Why would he have taken time off? He hadn't mentioned anything to me that day. Was he hiding something, or had something terrible happened?

I thanked the officer and called Oliver's sister next. Eva's elegance came through even on the phone, her voice suave and melodic. "He's not with you?" She sounded surprised, even a bit worried. "Where in heaven's name can he be?" My exact question.

Panic was rising in my throat, drowning me in a flood of hysterical thoughts and fears. "Why would he take time off? He didn't mention anything he was doing that day or the next. Now he's been missing for a whole day…."

"I'm sure there is a perfectly reasonable explanation." His sister seemed calm in spite of it all. "Oliver is a levelheaded guy. He wouldn't do anything crazy. I'll call the B and B and check. He may have gone up there again to clear his head." Her voice betrayed her. It was clear that even Eva thought that was a far-fetched idea. Oliver would have asked someone he trusted to drive him there, or at least made sure someone knew.

"Please, let me know." I felt tears burn behind my eyes. Something was terribly wrong. I had known it since the moment we said goodbye at his door as I fought against the urge to go up to his apartment with him. I'd had several errands to run and couldn't afford to give in to my instincts. We had kissed, long and hard, and then I watched him go in, cane in hand, until the door closed behind him. Ever since that moment this nasty aura had followed me around like a creepy stalker. I had tried to make sense of it unsuccessfully until now. Something foul had happened.

As soon as I hung up, I jumped to my feet and zoomed in the direction of my little kitchen. "Celia, something is very wrong. I need to find out what's going on." My brain was scouring my vast list of spells and enchantments for something I could use to figure it all out. "I need some candles. Help me find them."

A half-dazed Celia followed me to the kitchen. "What are you going to do?" Despite having no idea what I was about to do, my best friend immediately threw herself into the search for candles in my shelves.

"A tracking spell. I need colors for all the chakras." While Celia searched for a collection of candles, I pulled out my phone and searched for a picture of Oliver. "I think I have an old map of the area in a drawer." Opening and closing drawers helped me keep my mind off the terrible growing weight on my chest. Methodically I collected all the ingredients and materials needed for the spell, using all my powers of concentration to focus on the job at hand and not the fear in my heart.

At the last minute I ran to my laptop and printed eight pictures of Oliver. Under much protest I had taken several pictures of him and me during our weekend in the mountains. I couldn't be happier now for having pestered him about it. This spell would only work with his likeness in one form or another.

Celia helped me spread the old map on the floor of the store and went to turn the door sign to Closed while I placed the candles one at a time from east in a clockwise direction. My friend squeezed my shoulder before kneeling besides me. "What do we do now?"

"Now, we start lighting the candles and chanting the spell."

I lit a match and took a deep sigh. "By the fire of his soul, I call candlelight to guide me, so that Oliver must be found." I lit the red candle and carefully burned the first picture over it. I heard Celia echoing my words under her breath. I smiled at her to reassure her I was okay, even though my heart was hurting.

I repeated the ritual one step at a time until I had gone through most of the candles and the pictures. The ashes of what had been photos of Oliver's handsome face floated up in the air around us and I fought the urge to gather them all to me in an embrace. I had one more candle to burn. I struck another match and lit the purple candle after chanting the spell again, setting the last picture on fire on top of the map. The old yellowed paper caught and began burning slowly at first, the flames then quickening their track through it. I closed my eyes and thought of Oliver, conjuring a clear image of the man I loved in my mind. *This has to work. This has to work.* Never had I wanted a spell to work as much as this one.

"Marcy." Celia was next to me, shaking me gently. "It is all burned. Did you see it? Do you know where he is?"

Tears burned in my eyes. "Not yet." Every witch knew spells like this sometimes took some time to work, the answer to the question lying in the back of your awareness for a while before being perceived. I had to be patient and wait for my senses to open up to it. But the fear of losing Oliver made me impatient, unwilling to wait. I shook my head in frustration and anger. "Not yet."

Celia wrapped me in her arms and pulled me to her. "It will

come, Marcy. It will come." *It may be too late.* "You always get your man." We both laughed weakly at her attempt at a joke. "Come on. Let's go have a cup of tea."

I locked the store behind us and we walked down the street to the Old Bookstore. I wondered whether other people used that place as a comfort site, the one place you go to when you need to feel at home. We sat in our usual booth and ordered one hot cup of Oolong and a giant coffee concoction for Celia, the caffeine fiend. I couldn't help but smile at the white mustache Celia was wearing after a long sip of her whipped-cream-topped coffee. She placed her hand on top of mine and nodded. Yeah, I knew it would come to me eventually. The question was, would it be soon enough to help him? Because by now I was certain Oliver was in danger.

OLIVER

When you grow up with a monster for a father, there aren't that many things that will scare you senseless. The memories of his beatings and other of his chosen ways of physical and emotional torture were what scared me the most. Even losing my sight had not filled me with the terror those recollections did. I was scared now. Not because of the darkness that surrounded me. I was used to walking in darkness. But because I was alone. A sense of sheer panic was bubbling up my chest as I became more and more disoriented.

Blake had left me alone and without my cane. As soon as the sound of the car's engine faded into the distance, I felt it: The paralyzing fear that came from knowing you're lost. I didn't move for a while, afraid if I did I would fall to my death. I knew the area well since I used to come here on hikes and short weekend forays. But I could see then, and I was not alone. The small hotel on the cliff was always bubbling with visitors back then. You couldn't go too far without meeting another person. But the inn had closed a couple years ago, a grim symbolic event to mark the definite end to my marriage. Now there wasn't anyone, not a soul in this rather remote area of the pass. All the hotels and restaurants were miles away. I was alone.

After standing in the growing cold, still wearing the clothes I had worn to go meet with Marcy at the coffee shop, I began walking. With just a thin white shirt under a grey suit, no sweater, no warm coat, I felt half frozen already. I couldn't very well stand there all night hoping someone would come along to rescue me. They would find a human popsicle. I walked at the pace of a snail, unsure of my footing and of which direction I was heading. With nothing to guide me, I was like a boat adrift in the ocean. One step at a time, one foot in front of the other. My body shook violently, half from the cold seeping through my thin clothes, half from apprehension. What did I get myself into? Why did I trust Blake? Since when was she on the level? *Never, fool! She was never truthful.* And yet, I had accepted her invitation for a chat, I had even given her my phone in the car so she could call her lawyer. I walked blindly and willingly into her trap.

"Where are you taking me, Blake? This is not the way to your lawyer." Even though suspicion had been gnawing at me for the past fifteen minutes or so, I'd dismissed my doubts as pure foolishness, paranoia. But when the car kept moving away from the noise of the city I knew something was off.

"How would you know? You're blind." The spite in her voice made me shudder.

"I'm blind, not stupid." Even though I was beginning to feel I was. I had been a willing victim to her deception. "Where are you taking me?"

"Stop complaining. You'll find out when we get there." I sat in silence, trying to recognize sounds, some kind of markers that would feel familiar, but the more she drove, the fewer sounds I could hear. I smelled the pine trees and the frigid night air. We were heading up the mountains.

Once she stopped the car, she got out and opened the door for me. "We're here. Get out." The time for pretense was gone. Her voice didn't hide the contempt, the hate she held for me.

I was stronger than her, but she had hurt me before, years ago, when I still thought I needed to save my marriage at any cost. Letting it go would have been an admission of failure to my father. We had argued about her excessive spending and the depletion of our bank account. I threatened to freeze her bank account. Not that I would have done it, but I had to try something to stop her. In anger she'd pulled a knife from our kitchen counter and lunged at me. I was able to sidestep her, taking the brunt of the blade on the palm of my hand when I tried to take it away from her. Furious that I had been able to stop her attack, she had grabbed a bottle of wine from the counter and hit me across the face with it. I could have taken her down but I couldn't bring myself to fight my own wife. As much as I felt weak, standing almost helpless against her, I know I would have felt even worse should I have lifted a hand to hit her.

As soon as I was out of the car, she slammed the door closed. "Just for the record, I never loved you, Oliver." She spat the words at my face and then walked away. "Never. I stayed with you to be close to your father. Fuck the father, milk the son, my mother always said." It wasn't a shock to hear her say it. I had always suspected something unsavory was going on between my father and her. But I had no time to dwell on her words. I heard another slamming door, and then the sound of the engine. She was going to leave me there.

I scrambled toward the car, but it was too late. The tires squealed and a cloud of dirt hit my face as the car sped away. A bullet had not killed me. Was this going to be my demise?

With unsure footing, I advanced in the night, no clue as to where I was heading. For all I knew I was walking away from a possible rescue. I heard the owls and the rustling of leaves in the icy wind. Nothing else. *Marcy! Come save me.* Could the little witch hear me? We seemed so well attuned, I could almost believe she would indeed hear my plea. Distracted, I tripped over a rock and lost my balance.

I fell, and realized too late I was close to the edge of the precipice. My body hit the ground and rolled over the edge and into emptiness. The cold air the only thing holding me, I fell, rolling for a while, my mind conjuring all kinds of frightening scenarios as I bumped and crashed against branches and rocks on my way down. I felt my clothes rip and the freezing air seep through the open gaps to burn my skin. Was this how I was going to die? Alone and helpless? I continued to fall through the icy darkness for what seemed like forever, bracing myself for the final impact—the one I was certain would kill me. My body crushed into something solid and jagged. Sharp edges of rock cut into my flesh, but I couldn't scream. The impact took my breath away and I gasped for air before rolling and falling again. And again.

I must have passed out. When I came to later—no idea how much later—I knew my arm was out of commission and that I was bleeding from some wound in my chest or my belly. Maybe both. Everything hurt. With numb fingers I examined my shirt. It was shredded in several spots and damp with blood. The wind buffeted my already half-frozen body. I had to find some shelter. With whatever strength I had left, I dragged myself in no particular direction until I rolled down a slope again. This time it was a short fall, and the wind was not as punishing here. I felt around me for leaves, bushes, anything that I could wrap myself with or around for further protection from the cold. As my energy and strength fizzed away quickly, I closed my eyes and called Marcy again. With the faint hope she would somehow hear me, my consciousness faded away into oblivion.

Hypothermia & Hot Pads

MARCY

Frigid air was seeping under his clothes and he curled himself into a ball under a bush, gathering the fallen leaves and loose dirt around him to keep him warmer. His leg burned and he couldn't put weight on it without agonizing pain. He could smell the fresh scent of evergreens and hear the gurgling water of a nearby stream, but he had no way of knowing where he was exactly. There was no light anywhere. Night must have fallen. For a moment, Oliver allowed himself a moment of panic. With temperatures falling to the teens overnight, he was as good as dead if someone didn't find him soon.

I sat up in bed, eyes wide open and a sour taste in my mouth. The scent of the evergreens still clung to my nostrils, and in my ears the sound of flowing water still echoed. I knew where Oliver was. Not the exact place, but the vicinity.

I shook the sleeping Celia next to me. "Wake up, Celia. I know where he is." Celia mumbled something and slowly woke from her slumber. "We've got to go." I was already out of the bed, pulling on a pair of sweatpants over the ones I had on already. "Dress warmly. He's in the woods and he's hurt."

In less than ten minutes we were both dressed and ready to go. I had filled a thermos with Oliver's tea, hoping it would keep warm for a while. When I pulled a collection of camping supplies from my hallway closet, Celia frowned. "What are those for?"

"Oliver is lost in the mountains. We will need these." Celia knew better than to argue with my witch's logic. Not to boast, but I was not known for being wrong often. My instincts were normally on the money, even if sometimes a bit to the side. I had correctly predicted Jem and Em's kidnapping, even if not in detail. Much to my dismay sometimes, I always seemed to know when something bad was about to happen, and Celia had never doubted me. "Can you call Marc on our way there? Let him know what's going on?"

"I'm not sure how much he will be able to do on a hunch only—"

I turned sharply. "It's not a hunch!" The uncharacteristic anger in my voice made Celia flinch.

"I believe you, Marcy. You know that." It was a plea. "But others are different."

I sighed, already regretting my reaction. "I know, sorry for snapping at you." Resuming our way to the car,

I adjusted the heavy pack on my back. "But as soon as I pinpoint his location, you'll have to convince Marc to come to the rescue."

Celia followed me down the stairs. "I will. You know I will. Where are we going?"

"Oliver's mountains. He is lost and hurt in his mountains." My voice caught. It was hard not to notice the irony of the situation. Oliver was in danger of dying in the one place he had always felt safe and at home. And the one place that had always given me a strange sense of dread.

The drive up to the place where I had spent such a wonderful weekend with the man I loved seemed to take forever. Celia allowed me the silence I needed to get in tune with what we had always jokingly called my spidey senses, driving my car while I slumped on the passenger seat deep in thought. The feeling of foreboding was getting stronger and stronger in my chest, choking me. I twisted my hands in a mixture of fear and anger. What could have possibly taken over Oliver to get himself in a dangerous situation? Yes, he was a policeman, but he had been stuck to a desk for the past few months. Unless he had decided to get involved in something he shouldn't have. I could well believe Oliver would have jumped into some investigation he was not assigned to if he thought he could solve it. At the same time, he was so by-the-book, so straitlaced, it was hard to imagine he would go against the wishes and orders of his superiors.

The car had just begun a steep climb toward the bed and breakfast we had stayed at when the thought came to me, strong and clear. "Stop the car, Celia!" I needed stillness for a few seconds to make sense of what I had just *seen* with my third eye.

Without questioning me, my friend pulled the car off the road onto a narrow shoulder. "Did you see something? Do you know where he is?"

I closed my eyes, breathing deeply and purposefully, searching within my own thoughts for an answer. I could see him clearly, curled upon himself on the ground, shivering. I needed to see more. To find out where *this* was. To pinpoint Oliver's exact location. I took a few more breaths, my eyes still shut and my mind wide open. The smell of the evergreens and the slightly musty scent of wet leaves on the ground reached my nose. Oliver was very cold, the winter chill of the night air crossing the weak barrier of his clothes into his body underneath. There was a thin layer of snow on the ground, and the threat of more snow permeated the air. We needed to get to him fast.

"Let's go." Celia pulled out onto the deserted, dark road and resumed the ascent. "I don't know exactly where, but I have a general sense of where he may be. Just follow the road slowly and I will give you directions as I figure them out." My friend didn't argue, eyes trained on the darkness ahead.

When we came upon a fork on the road, I knew which way to go and, as we climbed further up and away from the foot of the mountain where the B and B was, my thoughts became more coalescent. With a certainty that astounded even me, I directed Celia to turn here and there, go right or left in an endless torrent of instructions.

"Here! Stop here." I heard it with my third eye, the weak but clear sound of Oliver's voice. *Talk to me love, please. Tell me where you are.* The voice was hard to understand and I had to strain my ears as if it were a real sound. I heard it again and again. "The pass!" Of course, he had mentioned having spent time in a hotel at the pass. Grabbing my phone, I began typing away. "Got to find where this hotel was."

"What hotel?" Celia had stopped the car by the side of the road and was staring at me as if I had grown two heads. "What are you talking about?"

My fingers continued tapping on the phone. "Oliver mentioned he came here a couple times with his wife and spent some time in a hotel at the pass. The hotel is closed now, but I'm sure there is information online about its location."

"Not to be the naysayer, Marcy, but why would he come to a closed hotel?" Celia was now biting her fingers and blinking at the speed of light.

"I don't know. I just know that that's what Oliver just told me." My friend stared at me, her mouth open. I licked my lips. I sometimes forgot other people couldn't experience what I often heard and saw in my head. "I just had a vision, Celia. Oliver said he was at the pass."

"The pass is rather huge," Celia said unhelpfully.

"I know that. That's why we are looking for the hotel's location. Considering that he has been here before, there is a good chance he is in the vicinity of the hotel." I could tell by her wide-open eyes that Celia didn't share the same faith in my logic, but there was no time to argue or explain things further. We needed to find him before he froze to death. My screen lit up and a picture of an abandoned small hotel popped up, along with an address. "Got it! Let's go, it's not too far from here."

Within the next fifteen minutes we had arrived at the old hotel, now a ghost of a building, dark and decrepit, perched at the top of a cliff. In the darkness, it looked as if it was in imminent danger of falling down into the base of the high rocky wall. As soon as Celia parked the car, I jumped out and ran to the ledge now devoid of its safety barriers.

"Be careful, Marcy!" Celia's voice was loud and echoed through the silence of the mountain.

Nose up in the air, I could smell snow coming as I peered down from my perch into the darkness below. Not quite sure of what I was looking for, I tightened my lips, refusing to feel discouraged. Armed with a strong flashlight from the car, I searched again, the beam of light moving slowly across the whole area below. That's when I noticed the faint glint of light, way below us, a reflection against something shiny.

"There! Do you see it?" I pointed down the gully at the bottom of the incline. Celia stared and made an excited sound when she saw it as well. "It has to be Oliver. The light is reflecting off his watch or something."

"What are we going to do?" Celia took her eyes off the bottom and looked at me with an expression of confusion. "That is awfully deep down there, and I don't see any paths or roads."

"There has to be a path down. This used to be a tourist destination. I'm sure there is something." I was on my phone again. "Shit! The signal is spotty."

Celia pulled out her phone and dialed a number. "Em, this is Celia." Celia frowned and rolled her eyes as she listened to her sister on the other end of the conversation. "I know it's late, dummy. This is an emergency. I'm going to text you an address of a hotel that's closed. I need you to find out whether there are any trails or paths down to the gully below." Celia brushed a hand across her face. "I can't get online because the signal is weak. We're in the mountains." More frowning and eye rolling. "I'll explain later. Just check and send me the info quick. Please, sis."

With a smile, I slid an arm over my friend's shoulders and pulled her against me. "Thank you, Celia. You're the best."

"Don't thank me yet. Let me send her the info." She worked on a text message while I walked around the hotel looking for some place that could lead down the side of the cliff. The vegetation was thick and hard to navigate in the dark. Celia called me back after a short while. "Em says there should be a walkway on the right side of the hotel that leads into some old trails. But the hotel has been closed for some years now, and the trails are probably grown over."

"I don't care. Better than tumbling down this mountain." I immediately turned around to collect the gear I had brought along. Celia helped me attach the giant backpack to my back and then followed me toward the hotel. "As soon as we find these trails you're going to go back to town and fetch Marc, okay?"

After a short search, we found the old trails, now overgrown with bushes, trees, and grass. It wouldn't be an easy walk down but it was the only way.

"Are you sure you'll be okay? I hate leaving you alone. I can call Marc instead." Celia seemed more than reluctant to abandon me. "I can stay in the car where it's warm—I've got plenty of gas—and call Marc from there. That way I will be close if something happens."

There was nothing wrong with her reasoning. "All right, that's fine. Just promise me you will not come down. You, my friend, have no outdoor skills whatsoever, and I don't need someone else to worry about." Celia laughed nervously. "Love you, Celia."

Celia gave me a quick hug and watched as I began my trek down the path, my hand raised to move bushes and branches that blocked the way. The vegetation closed behind me and soon I couldn't see Celia anymore. I hoped she had gone back to the car and called her boyfriend, but most of all I hoped she was safe. Celia was a spunky young woman, but she was very much a city girl. Me, on the other hand, I had learned the hard way how to survive in the great outdoors.

After I had lost my parents and entered the tumultuous world of foster care, I had run away a few times, unhappy with the guardians I had been assigned to. One foster parent had a heavy hand and did not need much provocation to use it, and another had suspiciously hungry eyes that often roamed my teen body when his wife wasn't looking. The woods had always been my go-to place, mostly because it was so vast and made searches that much more difficult and longer. But also because of the lack of human life. In my teen years, I had found humans tiresome and untrustworthy, making the prospect of a few days in the wild much more attractive. I had quickly learned how to survive.

It took me some time to get to the bottom of the incline. The trail was so overgrown that every step I took required removal of obstacles like branches, bushes, and rocks, slowing me down and making me anxious. Oliver was at the bottom in the freezing cold, hurt and alone with nothing to guide him to safety. A soon as I set foot at the bottom, I sped up the pace in the direction of where I had seen the glare. Easier said than done. The vegetation was not as thick here, but it was still hard to see around the giant evergreen trees and tall winter bushes. To complicate matters further, it had started snowing, a very light dusting of almost transparent snowflakes that melted as soon as they hit the ground. I knew this was just the beginning. The big snow was coming soon, and I had to get to Oliver before it did.

Without means of reference, it was hard to tell how much time had passed since I arrived at the bottom of the gully, but I was certain that if I followed its meandering up some ways, I would eventually come across Oliver. I didn't know how I could be so sure, but I was. The years had taught me to trust my instincts. As I navigated a particularly sharp turn in the trench, I finally saw him.

"Oliver!" The scream came out before I was even aware. I ran as fast as I could, weighted down by the huge backpack, toward the figure lying ahead. He didn't move and suddenly I feared the worst. "Oliver, it's me. I'm here now. Hold on."

My knees hit the frozen ground hard, and had I not been

so worried about the man lying before me, I would have winced in pain. My hands went to his neck to check for a pulse but before I could even do it, I noticed his shivering. Oliver's body was shaking convulsively, as if he had lost total control of his muscles.

"Thank all the stars. You're alive." I was whispering, afraid of adding to his obvious discomfort with loud noises. After unloading the backpack, I turned Oliver's body around to see his face. It was hard to tell by the faint light of the moon whether his skin color was off, but the constant knocking of his teeth told me he was suffering from hypothermia already. Blood stained his forehead and the right side of his face "Oliver, can you hear me?" I placed my hand on his icy cheek and carefully examined the wound on his head. It felt superficial, skin deep. I sighed in relief.

Oliver moved, his eyes fluttering open. "Marcy? Is that you?" His voice was choppy and unsteady, so unlike his usual. "Am I dreaming?"

"No, you're not dreaming. It's really me." I opened the backpack and removed a blanket, which I carefully tucked around Oliver's body. "You're going to be okay. I'm going to warm you up."

A strange gurgling sound came out of Oliver and for a moment I thought he was choking. Surprised, I realized he was laughing. "Fierce little witch, I don't doubt it for a moment. Looking forward to it." The chattering of teeth made it hard to understand what he was saying at first, but I had to smile. It was a good sign that he had not lost his sense of humor.

While Oliver shivered away in the cocoon of the warm blanket, I got busy setting up camp. I checked my phone but, just as I had predicted, there was no signal down here. With cold fingers, I untied the sleeping bag I'd brought with me, an impulse buy of a few years ago when I had attended a survival weekend in the mountains. This was not your average sleeping bag. Once you unrolled it, it became an "instant" tent, insulated against the cold and the elements. It was small and we would be crowded inside, but considering Oliver was in extreme need of heat, that wasn't a bad thing. There was nothing like the heat from another body cuddled tightly against you. A few minutes later it was ready. I extracted some hand warmers from my backpack, a thermos of hot tea, and a water bottle and placed them strategically on top of the sleeping bag.

I returned my attention to Oliver, lying right beside me. "Oliver, do you think you can move enough to scoot to the sleeping bag next to you?" Oliver tried to speak, but his chattering teeth wouldn't let him. "All right. I'm going to help you by rolling you into it, okay?"

Slowly, I positioned myself on his other side, and putting all my weight into it, I pushed until I felt Oliver's body turn. He moaned weakly. His whole body was taken by the shakes, which made it more difficult, but slowly Oliver made his way to the bottom of the sleeping bag, wincing in pain with each move. I picked up the discarded blanket, closed the backpack, and positioned it against the side of the gully. Before crawling in next to Oliver I looked around, studying my surroundings. Being inside the gully had its benefits but also a downside. It kept us sheltered from the wind, but once it started snowing in earnest we could quickly get buried in it. I would cross that bridge when I got there. Right now the priority was to get Oliver warmed up before his hypothermia became more severe.

"Don't get too excited, but I'm going to crawl in here with you." I was hoping a little joking would lift up his spirits. It worked. He laughed softly between the clicking sounds of his jaws hitting each other. I stretched myself carefully alongside him and pulled the insulated dome over us. We were suddenly immersed in total darkness. A quick rummage through my pockets yielded a small LED flashlight. "A little light so I can see your handsome face."

"Thank you for finding me." Oliver chuckled again, belying the look of pain on his face. "How *did* you find me?"

I was glad he was talking, even if through the castanet sound of his trembling jaws, but I was not done yet. I broke the seal on several hand warmers and placed one on his neck. "I'm a witch, remember? Do you believe me now? Hold these." I handed him two more warm pads.

"I can't feel my fingers." That was worrisome. Hopefully the heat would counteract the lack of blood circulation into his extremities. With difficulty he held the pads and I helped him close his fingers around them. He moaned. "I never doubted your magic powers, you know."

I laughed, inserting another warm pad underneath his shirt. "This one is going under your armpit." I shuffled around a little more. It was difficult to move in such a cramped space, but the heat from our bodies huddled together was beginning to take the punch out of the cold air. "Celia is calling the police to come and help us out of this hole."

"Marc? She called Marc?" His voice sounded hopeful, a little color returning to his face in the dim light.

"Yes." I broke the seal on the last hand warmer and shook it. "You're going to love this one. I need to stick it inside your pants."

The sound of his laughter, now less shaky, made my heart jump for joy. "What a strange time for you to be having these kind of thoughts, little witch. Even if I wanted, I doubt that part of my body is functioning properly right now."

I laughed and without any further warning, unzipped his pants and slid a warmer pad between his legs. "We'll see about that later."

Pulling the blanket over both of us, I settled curled up against his side, careful not to hurt him further, my head on his chest. Oliver was alive and relatively well. I could hear the beat of his heart strong against my cheek, and it warmed me up inside and out.

"Marcy…."

"Yes?" It felt warm and cozy in his arms even though his body was cold and still shivering.

"I love you."

This time, I didn't hesitate. "I love you too."

OLIVER

Was it possible to have stars in your body? I could have sworn a million stars had descended from the sky and taken up residence in my left arm. They twinkled and burned, tiny little suns away from home.

I could feel Marcy by my side, cuddled against me, her body absorbing the coldness of mine. Could she feel my stars? If I squinted I could even see them, glittering in the corner of my vision. If I tried to focus on them, they ran and hid, like mischievous children in a game of tag.

The cold still tugged at my body like long icy fingers, pulling me down into the depths of a dark ocean of snow. Wait! Snow was not dark. I laughed at my own thoughts.

So cold… was that me shivering? And why couldn't I feel my left hand? I wanted to touch it with my other hand, but Marcy was lying on it, so I tried to wiggle my fingers instead. Nothing.

I was so cold.

The wind was singing outside. Or yelling. Hard to say for sure.

So cold….

The stars in my arm had climbed up to my eyes. I could see them on my eyelids, pretty and shiny, expanding and taking over.

So cold….

MARCY

Her wiry body floated above us like a dark wisp of smoke, her bluish face contorting into a frown and her long hair flapping in the wind behind her. I could see her approaching, her terrible red eyes shining in the dark, sharp teeth framing her gaping mouth. Her horrific screeches surrounded us and pierced my ears.

"You, you...," she howled, echoing all the way into my bones. I held on tighter to Oliver, shivering in my arms, afraid the banshee was coming to take him away.

"No, no. You can't have him." Within the cocoon of my embrace, Oliver was shaking so hard it felt like an earthquake was rocking us.

I woke up. The wind was howling outside our sleeping bag tent, jerking it this way and that way. I reached out to touch Oliver's face and was startled by how cold he still felt. I lifted myself on one arm and began frantically checking the rest of his body. As my hands slipped inside his shirt, I was shocked to find it damp. *How didn't I notice that before?* Hypothermia and moisture of any kind did not go well together. Tremors were rocking his body and his skin felt cold.

"Oliver, Oliver." I needed to know he was still conscious. I struggled with the buttons of his shirt. Why was he wearing a suit? Why would he come to the mountains dressed like this? "Oliver, help me get rid of your shirt."

A faint movement told me he could hear me. His voice was weak and slurred, but he was still speaking. "I admire your enthusiasm, Marcy, but I told you, I'm in no condition for sex." Silly man. Still trying to make jokes even when it was obvious his strength was sapped to the bare minimum.

With great difficulty I managed to open up his shirt. I pointed the light at his chest and barely kept from screaming. A giant abrasion crossed his whole chest and abdomen, staining it with blood. I brushed my fingers along the wound. I didn't have any medical training, but it seemed as if the wound was not too deep. The bleeding had stopped some time ago, for it was mostly coagulated—except for the part dampening the shirt. I was not going to be able to turn him around, so I fished the scissors out of my first aid packet, cut around the wet surface, and used the cut fabric to soak up as much moisture as I could from the wound. The heat pads were still warm, so I repositioned one under his arm and squeezed myself as close as I could get to him, my arms wrapped around his body, feeling his heart beat against mine.

"You smell good." His voice was so faint I almost didn't hear it. I snuggled against him, my head cradled in the crook of his neck. He smelled good, too. Even out here, hypothermic and bloody, his usual fresh scent filled me with a soothing sense of peace. He smelled of pine trees and bubbling creeks. I drifted off to sleep, hoping the banshees would leave me be this time.

Light seeping through the metallic material of the tent woke me up sometime later. For the first time since I had arrived, I could see clearly, even inside the shelter. Nestled against me, Oliver still shivered, the twitches not as pronounced as before but still a worry. Carefully I lifted the edge of the canopy and saw with dismay that it was snowing. The tiny flakes fell profusely if not heavily all round us, covering the ground with a thin white mantel. Hopefully we would be rescued soon, before the snow got heavy enough to bury us in the ditch.

I crawled out of the tent, being careful not to allow too much icy air to sneak in, and stretched. My muscles were sore and cramped from the lack of movement and the cold temperatures. I retrieved the backpack from where I had left it and began removing more heat pads and another blanket. I had brought some of his special tea in a thermos, but I doubted it was still warm. Nevertheless, Oliver should take a few sips of it before his hallucinations became worse. He didn't need that on top of his injuries and hypothermia.

Oliver was moving when I went back in, fighting with the blanket I had wrapped tightly around him the night before. "Oliver, stop. It's okay. I'm here."

He stopped fidgeting for a moment. "Is that you, Marcy? Am I hallucinating?" I flipped the edge of the sleeping bag and crawled in next to him. "You feel real."

I giggled. "I'm glad, because I *am* real." I unscrewed the top of the thermos and was relieved to feel a faint waft of warm air hit my face. The tea was not completely cold after all. I lifted Oliver's head just enough for him to take a sip. "Here's your tea. It's probably just lukewarm, but you need it."

Obediently Oliver took a couple of sips and sighed. "Not to alarm you or anything, but I can't feel my left hand. Is that normal?" I almost dropped the container. *No, it is not normal.*

In my rush to dig up his arm from underneath the blanket, I almost dropped the tea. I replaced the cap on the thermos and set it aside. "Let me check your arm." The skin on his forearm was a strange mottled grayish color, but the most alarming thing was the swelling. The whole area below the elbow was twice its normal size. A gasp escaped my lips.

"What? What's wrong?" Shit, now he would be worried. No point in getting him anxious about this.

"Does it hurt when I move it?" I slid my hand under his arm and tried to lift it up a few inches. Oliver screamed in pain. "I guess that's a yes." The arm must be broken. The good news was that the bone was not sticking out of his skin, but the swelling pointed at a bad break. He needed urgent medical attention. "It may be broken, Oliver. Try not to move it."

Oliver turned his beautiful eyes to me and laughed. "No problem there, little witch. I have no wish to feel that again."

Should I apply ice to his arm? Was that the right thing to do for a broken bone? But Oliver was still mildly hypothermic. If I applied ice—of which there was plenty outside right now—to his arm, his body temperature would drop again. I searched in my mind what the doctors in TV medical shows I had watched throughout the years had done for broken bones. *It's only fiction, Marcy.* But most were based on real medical research. Or so I hoped at the moment.

"Splint it." It was Oliver. I stared at his bloodied face with a question in my eyes. He couldn't see me, but he must have read my mind. "To make sure it does not move, you have to splint it."

Once again I stared at him stupidly. "I don't know how to do that." I could possibly come up with a spell to alleviate his pain, but coming up with a splint was not in my list of skills.

"Do you have a big book or thick magazine with you?" *I didn't exactly plan on a leisurely time here in the mountains, Oliver.* But I did have something like that in the backpack; an old book of spells I had forgotten to take out of the backpack. "You can use it for a splint. I'll help you."

With the book of spells now in my hand, I closed the dome around us again. Because of its height I couldn't stand or even sit straight. Hunching like an old hag was not agreeing with my back, not to mention it made for very awkward movement. "What do I do now?"

"Open the book in the middle and carefully sandwich my forearm with it." People complained about witchcraft all the time, but was medicine all that different? Sandwiching a broken arm with a book seemed like something out of a novel. "You're going to need a scarf or some cloth to wrap around it."

I did as he told me, gingerly touching his arm and wincing every time he moaned in pain. The scarf I was wearing would have to do as a bandage of sorts, so I unwound it from my neck and began wrapping it around the book. "Is this okay?"

Oliver examined my work with his fingers and smiled. "You're doing a great job, little witch. Tie it at the ends and see if it stretches around my shoulder to make a sling."

By the time I was finished I felt I had run a marathon.

The pressure of doing something I had never done before was amplified by my fear of hurting Oliver more than he already was. I noticed his face was still stained in his own blood. "What should I do about your head wound and face scratches?"

"Do I look like Frankenstein then?" His lips stretched into a big smile. I knew he was only being brave because of me. He had to be in great pain. Not only did he have that broken bone, but he had also suffered several abrasions on his head, face, and body. The smile died on his lips. "Was I dreaming, or did you tell me you loved me?"

My heart flip-flopped. Why was telling the one you loved how you felt so scary? What was I afraid of exactly? "I did." I was not sure I had spoken loud enough for him to hear me.

His good hand reached out from under the blanket to grasp my hand resting on his belly. "You've made me a very happy man."

I slid down inside the bag and held him to me. "I do love you, Oliver. I love you very much."

We lay in silence for a while. It occurred to me I hadn't asked him why and how he had ended up on the bottom of that gully.

"My ex-wife. She's the one who brought me here." Could he read my mind? He was always so attuned to what I was thinking. It was spooky, even for a witch.

"Blake did this? Why?"

"She called me at the precinct and asked me if I would go with her to her lawyer to discuss the terms of our impending divorce." Oliver's voice was steadier, but I noticed his body still shook sporadically. "At first I said no, but in the end I figured we needed to talk at some point. I called my lawyer and asked him to meet us there. She picked me up at my place first thing, the morning after we met at the café. After driving for almost an hour, I became suspicious. Her lawyer's office is less than forty-five minutes from my house."

I scooted closer to him, listening to his story. Blake was even more evil than I had given her credit for. She had driven to the pass, which she knew was not frequently visited anymore now that the hotel was closed, and had left Oliver by the side of the road after tricking him into exiting the car. Her intentions were clear; she knew that Oliver could not find his way into town by himself. With the night falling and the temperatures dropping, she knew he didn't stand a prayer. He would either fall off the edge where she had left him or he would die of exposure.

"What about your phone? Couldn't you have called?" I knew the signal was spotty in the mountains but a text may have gone through.

"Before we got here she asked to use my phone under the pretense she had forgotten hers at home. Needless to say, she never gave it back to me." Oliver was silent for a while. Temperatures were still falling. I could feel the tips of my hands beginning to tingle. Where were Celia and Marc? "I was disoriented from the long drive and getting very cold. But I had to do something. I couldn't stand there all night hoping someone would drive by."

Oliver had tried to get his bearings and follow the road,

but he missed his footing and fell over the edge. Thankfully he rolled rather than plummeted down the hill, being stopped here and there by bushes and branches. Even though they battered and scratched him, the obstacles on his way down had slowed his fall and ultimately saved his life.

"Once I was on the bottom I passed out for a bit. Not sure how long." I shivered against him, anger growing inside my chest. The woman was pure evil. It wasn't as if she would be destitute after the divorce, since Oliver had made sure she would be well provided for. Why kill? Where did this need for more come from? I had never been able to wrap my head around the greed and anger that often led to murder, but I supposed that only meant I was not one of those people.

Hurt and freezing, Oliver had dragged himself around until he dropped a couple feet into the gully. "At least here I was more protected from the wind." He was quiet again and I felt his lips on the top of my head. "I called you, Marcy. I called you in my dreams and you came."

Tears welled up in my eyes. "I heard you, Oliver." I was overwhelmed by the fact that we had this connection. That I could hear him across the miles. Even in my witch experience, I had never felt this connected to anyone. My heart swelled and I felt warm all over even in the icy air. "Celia and Marc will be here anytime." I had checked my phone but there was still no signal. This gully was a dead zone.

"You're shivering." Oliver's voice seemed to come from far away, and I realized I was dozing off. My extremities were numb and tingly. *Not good.* I was beginning to slip into hypothermia as well.

Remembering the extra hot pads I had brought from the backpack, I sprang into action—well, I moved into it. There was no way anyone could *spring* in that tight space. I snapped the seal on a couple more packs, slid one inside my shirt and under my arm, unrolled the extra blanket over the two of us, and then, giggling in spite of our rather dire situation, placed the last pack inside Oliver's pants and between his legs.

"You're incorrigible." Oliver chuckled and snuggled closer. The heat from the pad began spreading from my armpit to the rest of my body in a comforting way. I sighed in relief and allowed myself a moment of peace.

Whatever happened next, I thanked the heavens above and all the deities known to mankind for having thrown Oliver into my life. Even if it meant we were both going to die in that frozen ditch.

Rescue Missions & Hospital Gowns

MARCY

Sounds all seemed to be coming through a tunnel, and try as I may to open my eyes, they refused to do so; eyelids as heavy as lead and a head that felt as if it was magnetically being pulled toward the ground. Hands slipped under my arms and lifted me up. From a distance I heard Oliver moan in pain, and I whimpered in response. I wanted to struggle, to rid myself of whoever was holding and carrying me. I needed to be by Oliver's side, to make sure I shared my body heat with him, to keep him alive. *Wait, I'm so cold. Why am I so cold and numb?* Red pain shot inside my head as I was shaken, my feet dangling in the air.

"It's okay, Marcy." Celia's voice felt oddly out of place there but a comfort anyway. "We're taking you both to the hospital right now. Hang on, friend." A warm hand held my frozen one, and it felt like heaven.

"Oliver?" Was that my voice? Or had I just said that in my head?

"He's hurt and has hypothermia, but he's going to be okay. You're both going to be all right." Why did the hushed tone of her voice belie her words? Celia's strangled words told me we weren't really out of the woods quite yet. I could always tell when my friend was worried. She'd spoken in the same way when her sister was kidnapped. I was the one doing the hand-holding then. "Hang on, Marcy, please."

I'm not quite sure what happened after that, because the next thing I knew I was in a hospital bed, covered in a million blankets from head to toe, shaking convulsively within the warm cocoon. "I'm so-o co-o-old." It was hard to articulate any words when my jaws were snapping together, out of control. I could feel the wonderful warmth of the heated blankets, but my body was frozen inside. My eyes finally opened, found Celia standing by me, an anxious expression in her eyes, her hands grasping at invisible threads in her shirt. "Ce-elia."

"You're suffering from hypothermia, honey." The nurse placed another heated blanket over me. "We're trying to regulate your body temperature."

"God, Marcy. You guys almost froze out there." Celia's lips were twisted into a quivering frown as she leaned over me. "You could have died."

I tried to smile, but I was pretty sure I was only able to achieve a weird grimace, my body was shaking so hard. "But I di-didn't." A thought popped into my mind, and my heart, slowly pumping much needed blood to warm up my body, sped up. "Oliver? Wh-where is he?" *Is he alive? Is he all right?*

Celia sat on the edge of the bed, her hand tucking the blankets around me. "He's in surgery." My eyes opened wide and I shook even harder. "No worries. He'll be okay. The break was quite bad and he needed surgery to repair it. But he's okay otherwise. You managed to control his hypothermia, and the doctors said that the splint you applied on his arm saved him from further injury." She smiled, a little tremor at the corner of her lips betraying the tears I knew were burning in her eyes.

"Celia, I need you to bring me an amethyst crystal from the store." It was a healing stone and both Celia and I were in need of healing of body and soul. Sending her on an errand would distract her and make her feel less helpless. I knew that feeling was the worst part of worrying about those we loved. "We need to do a healing spell for Oliver."

Marc, whom I hadn't noticed was in the room, stepped forward and smiled. "I'll take her to your store." His hands rested on Celia's shoulders, protective and comforting. "Did Oliver tell you who did this to him?"

Had he been unconscious since the rescue? "His wife, Blake." My shaking had finally subsided enough that I could speak without stuttering. I could feel the warmth from the blankets seeping through my skin into my cold bones. "Blake Dawson."

Another nurse stepped in the room. "There is an Eva Dawson wanting to see you. Do you want to talk to her?"

Yes, I so wanted to talk to her. "Celia, get my crystal, please. I feel a lot better now, I promise. By the time you come back I will be dancing around the nurses." Celia laughed and left the room with Marc, crossing paths with the beautiful Eva.

"What the hell happened, Marcy?" She wasted no time with niceties. I was sure she was worried sick about her brother. "What the fuck was Oliver doing in the mountains alone? Did you have anything to do with that?"

"No, of course not." I should have been a little offended by her suggestion, but I knew how she was feeling. People in pain often felt the need to point fingers, even if in the wrong direction. "Blake left him to die." I wasn't going to waste any time either.

Her already milky-white complexion paled even further. "Blake? Blake did this to him?" Her usual composure was gone, fury evident in her eyes and the way she wrenched her hands. "That bitch!"

"How's Oliver? Is he out of surgery yet?" I missed him already. It felt as if a part of me was missing, and I wanted it back.

Eva composed herself, pulling on the sides of her impeccable blue suit jacket. She pulled a chair closer to the bed and sat down. "He's in the recovery room." She stared down at her hands and then up at me again. "Thank you, Marcy. They told me you most likely saved his life. I'll never be able to thank you enough. Sorry if it sounded like I was blaming you."

I sat up so fast my head swam. "I don't blame you. In fact, I know just how you feel because I feel the same way." Should I tell her? Why not? "I love your brother, and the thought that anyone wished him harm makes my blood boil." I giggled at my own surprise. "If you knew me better you'd know that doesn't happen very frequently or easily."

"True. She really is very Zen." It was Celia, leaning against the doorway, her arms crossed and a smile on her lips. "Marcy has the biggest heart I know."

Eva twisted her neck around to look at the newcomer. I laughed. "You make me sound like a saint, which I am definitely not."

Celia stepped in the room and came to sit on the edge of the bed, taking my hand in hers. "I came to tell you both that Oliver is awake."

Both Eva and I snapped our chins up. "Can I see him?" Eva asked. Celia looked at me as if asking for permission. I nodded. Eva was Oliver's sister. She should have the chance to speak to him first.

"The nurse said he's still very groggy, but yes, you can see him." Celia gave my hand an approving squeeze.

Eva stood up, her tall and slim body a bundle of coils. "Thank you." I was not sure whether she was thanking me for keeping her brother alive or for letting her see him first. I lifted my hand in a little wave and she left.

"You're dying to see him, aren't you?" Celia knew me well. Inside me the yearning was growing by leaps and bounds. Yes, I wanted to see Oliver's handsome face, get lost in his smoky blue eyes, and kiss him within an inch of his life. "You'll get your chance, but now you're mine. I sent Marc to get your crystals so I could stay with you." She squeezed my hand again and arched an eyebrow in a perfect imitation of an evil cartoon villain. "Spill! Did you guys get really cozy up there?"

I had to laugh. I knew she was not serious—at least not completely. Celia was trying to distract me from the fact that the man I loved was recovering from a surgery after being the victim of attempted murder. I played along. "We had to. For survival purposes, of course."

Marc found us lying side by side on the hospital bed, Celia lulled to sleep by my retelling of Oliver's trial, her head on the pillow next to mine. The burly red-haired policeman smiled and winked at me from the door. He lifted his hand in the air and quietly showed me the amethyst crystal I had requested. I smiled back, mouthing a silent thank-you. After what had happened, it felt heavenly to spend time with my best friend.

OLIVER

"Is he going to be okay?" The voice was not mine but I couldn't quite place it either. Familiar, though.

I was not sure where I was, but it was warm and that's all it mattered to me. My body had a vivid and unpleasant memory of being extremely cold. This was wonderful. Except… where was Marcy? My heart skipped a beat, my breath accelerating in panic. "Marcy…." My scratchy throat made it difficult to speak.

"She's okay." Familiar, so familiar. The fuzz in my brain tried to reorganize itself into some coherent shape, but it was hard to make sense of anything. What was happening to me?

"You're still woozy because of the anesthesia, Oliver. Take it easy."

Eva! That voice belonged to my sister. I tried to open my eyes but an elephant seemed to have sat on them. *Not that it would do me any good.* The dust bunnies in my head were clearing and I remembered with some measure of disappointment that I was still blind, and opening my eyes was not going to change anything. With more effort than it should have taken, I relaxed into the warmth of the bed and allowed myself to slowly come to my senses again.

"Where's Marcy?" A terrible sense of doom filled my heart every time I thought about what may have happened to my little witch.

"Marcy is fine. A little worse for the wear, but just fine." Eva's voice shook. Had she been crying? "You, on the other hand, nearly died. When the police catch up to Blake, I'm going to poke her eyes out with my own fingers."

The anger in her voice was so thick and real, I inhaled sharply in surprise. My sister was not an angry individual. "Whoa, Eva, let the law take care of her." I was pretty angry myself, but not at Blake. I was mad at myself for once again, and despite knowing she was psychotic, allowing myself to be the butt of her schemes, for giving in to her lies. "Marc will get her, and then you can indict her. She won't stand a chance."

Eva fell silent and I may have fallen asleep for a moment. "You should keep her." My eyes flew open at the sound of her voice, quiet and serious.

"Keep who?" She couldn't mean Blake, could she?

"Marcy, stupid!" I almost laughed at her use of the word. I couldn't even remember when she last talked to me like that. "Hold on to the witch. She saved your freaking stupid butt up there."

I laughed, my throat complaining with every chuckle. "I have no intention of letting her go. I love her." This was a day for firsts. Not that long ago I would never have admitted that to anyone close to me. In my experience, revealing feelings to family meant giving them a weapon against me. Not that my sister had ever been against me or had in any way hurt me, but she also hadn't done anything about the one who had caused me so much pain. Neither had my mother. "But I am surprised you approve."

"I didn't think she was the right match for you, but…." She sighed. "I've changed my mind. She's a good one, Oliver."

For some reason those few words from my sister made me hysterically happy. Marcy was my twin soul, and I would never let her go.

MARCY

Even in a hospital bed, scratched and bruised, Oliver looked strong and handsome. My heart overflowed with love as I watched him from the doorway. For someone who had never loved before, I sure had fallen hard and completely.

"Are you just going to stand there and stare, little witch?" Somehow it didn't surprise me he knew I was there. He seemed to have some sort of sixth sense when it came to me.

I laughed and stepped into the room. "How do you do that? It's kind of spooky." I made my way to his bedside, my heart thumping in my chest.

"This from a witch? I thought you believed in that kind of stuff!" Feigning disbelief, Oliver fidgeted in bed, trying to sit up. I hurried to help him prop up the pillows behind him. His arm was still attached to an IV, and he had a large bandage on his forehead. "Where have you been?" His voice dropped an octave as he closed his hand around my wrist.

The heat of his hand made my skin tingle. "Hiding in my room with Celia." *Missing you.* "I wanted to give your sister time to be with you alone. Did you guys have a good visit?" I sat on the edge of the bed, my eyes roaming over Oliver. His arm was in a cast and in a suspended sling. "Does your arm hurt? What did they do to it?"

"Whoa, girl. That's a lot of questions." He chuckled, his hand quickly seeking mine over the sheets. I slid my hand toward his until our fingers interlaced. A soothing warmth ran up my arm and into my whole body. "How are you feeling? They told me you got hypothermia also."

I shook my head and my messy curls, tangled from lying in bed, flew around my face. "It was nothing. You know these medical people; they make a whole lot out of very little." The twist of his lip told me he didn't believe me for a minute. "Unlike you and your broken arm. I hear you now have a nice metal plate in your forearm." I smiled for emphasis, even though I knew he couldn't see it.

"No more metal detectors for me." He laughed out loud. "I can only imagine the racket it will make every time I go to court to testify." I chuckled, even though I didn't find the fact that he now had a metal bar holding his arm bone together very funny at all.

"Did the police come to talk to you about Blake?" I had been so worried about Oliver, I had never once thought about what the police were doing about catching his would-be murderer. Celia told me that Oliver's ordeal was all over the news. Not only was he the son of a high-profile lawyer, but he was also a "human interest" story, the blind cop who did not allow his disability to rule his life. Blake must have seen it by now and realized how much trouble she was in.

"Marc was here to take a statement from me." His voice lost the playful tone. "He told me she was nowhere to be found, but they are looking."

I also lowered my voice, a bit hesitant. "And your parents? Have they been here?"

Oliver's lip quivered subtly. "No. Eva says Father is in the middle of a huge case and couldn't come down from DC to see me. And Mother does nothing without dear Father." His voice, thick with sarcasm, caught in his throat. "I wouldn't be surprised if my father is the one hiding my wife."

My head snapped up and I studied his face, trying to figure out whether he really believed that. He did. "Surely not."

"You don't know my parents. My father is Blake's biggest fan. I used to think that if it wasn't for the fact he's already married, he would marry her himself." Oliver grunted, bitterness bubbling to the surface. "It's a miracle both Eva and I turned out so reasonably well-put-together."

The weight in my hospital gown pocket when I shifted reminded me of the crystals I was carrying. "Almost forgot, Oliver. I brought some amethyst for your speedy recovery." The skin around his eyes crinkled in doubt. "Amethyst has amazing healing powers." I pulled the beautiful purple crystal from my pocket and placed it in the palm of his hand, closing his fingers around it. "Hold it tight and follow my lead."

Oliver opened his mouth to argue but thought better of it, and silence fell around us. I closed my eyes while wrapping my fingers around his fist and focused on my breath. A few moments later, when peace washed over me in a refreshing wave I cleared my throat gently. "Archangel Michael, patron saint of police officers, come to our rescue in this time of need." I felt Oliver twitch slightly but he remained silent. "I thank you for everything you have done for Oliver and me; for placing us in each other's path and sending rescuers our way. We are eternally grateful and always will be."

A big sigh escaped my lips before I continued my prayer. "Please protect him from the evil being wrought against him. Surround him with love and happiness and keep him safe from all wrongs." In my mind I built a magical cocoon with which I enveloped Oliver's body and spirit, a protective shield from my heart to his. "Help him heal and help him succeed." I closed the spiritual cocoon around him. "Thank you, angel of goodness, thank you for your love and protection." A sudden whoosh in my chest told me the spell was completed and the shield intact. I released his hand and immediately felt bereft.

"What did you just do?" Oliver sounded subdued, his eyes turning to me as if he could see me. I supposed in a way he could.

"Built a protective shield around you." I yearned to crawl in bed and snuggle against him, but I didn't think the nurses would be too happy. "I really want to kiss you right now." Okay, that was a bit random, but true nevertheless.

Oliver laughed again, an expression of relief on his face, as if he was happy to be back to a subject he could easily identify with. Unlike magic. "Then what are you waiting for, little witch?"

I leaned over the bed, my legs shaking a little in the aftermath of the incantation, and melded my lips to his. It felt good. Better than good. It felt as if I had just arrived home after a long absence. I may have swooned a little. "Love the way you taste."

"You are aware I haven't brushed my teeth in days, right?" The playful tone was back in his voice. His fingers were buried in my tangled hair, and the cool draft I was feeling on my behind told me my hospital gown had come undone. I didn't care. Being lip to lip with Oliver eclipsed all else, even the potential embarrassment of being caught mooning visitors and hospital staff.

Good News & Looming Threats

Marc: "The bitch has landed."

The cryptic text message made me smile. I had no idea what he meant, but I couldn't help being amused at his usual brass.

I dialed his number with my good hand, curious. "Marc? What the hell are you talking about?" I could hear the familiar bustling noises of business as usual at the precinct in the background.

"We got her!" I hesitated, still not sure what he meant. "The bitch. Blake, the psycho wife. We have her in custody." My legs buckled under me and I felt for the chair behind me. "She was living on a friend's yacht with plans to sail out in the next week or so."

I was almost afraid to ask. "Did my father have anything to do with hiding her?" Deep down, I didn't want to believe it, but my knowledge of my father told me otherwise.

"Hard to say. She's not talking." Because my father must have somehow promised her something in return for her silence in this matter. "But the important thing is we got her, and no lawyer in this world is going to save her." Marc was overly optimistic. He didn't know lawyers like I did. The fact that I was blind could and most likely would be used to shed enough doubt on my testimony to turn a sure-shot conviction into a reasonable doubt verdict.

"What now?" My arm, resting loosely in a sling, ached with the sudden tension in my muscles. "What do I do?"

"You do nothing, bro." Marc guffawed. "You get better so you can come back to work and then testify when the trial goes to court." His voice turned conspiratorial. "In the meantime, you enjoy Marcy's company and go shopping for her birthday. A ring may be a nice gift." He snorted, obviously amused by his own suggestion. "See? I can be fucking proper when I want to." I laughed and said my goodbyes just as the doorbell rang.

"It's me." Eva. I pressed the button to open the building front door and waited for her to come up the stairs. "I don't get why there is no elevator in this place." I could hear her labored breath as she came into my apartment.

"There are only three floors, and I'm only on the second." Eva was usually in good shape, exercising like an athlete for hours every week. I had always wondered whether she did that as an alternative for therapy. God knew all Dawson progeny would need therapy at some point in their lives. "You sound winded. Out of shape?"

"Let me sit down first." For a moment I actually worried

about her. She sounded really out of sorts. "I climbed too fast, that's all. Give me a minute."

I pulled a chair to sit by her. "You heard? About Blake?"

"Yes, that's why I'm here." Her breath was quickly going back to normal. "Are you okay?"

"I'm fine." A little shaken maybe, but all right. I adjusted the sling. My arm was healing nicely, but I still had a long way to go. It was strange to think I had two metal clamps holding my forearm bone together, but you had to admire and be grateful for modern medicine. "Can't wait to put this whole mess behind me."

"Well, I bring you even better news." I heard the rustling of papers. "I brought the final divorce papers for you to sign. The lawyer already got Blake's signature." I froze. Was she serious? Did she really have the papers sealing my freedom from my murderous wife? Papers I had waited for, for over two years. "Did you hear me? You're free."

My reaction surprised even myself. Wrapping my arm around my sister, I pulled her to me and cried on her shoulder. As I shed tears of happiness and relief, Eva squeezed me tightly against her and, I suspect, cried a little as well. "Thank you, Eva. You've made me a very happy man." I wiped my tears with the back of my hand, hoping I hadn't ruined the usually pristine look of my sister's clothes. "Did I mess up your shirt?"

"God, no." Her choked voice made me even happier. Getting close to my sister was definitely a huge silver lining of this horrid situation. "Nothing a good cleaner can't handle." I laughed, my divorce papers now in my hand. "I have something else to tell you."

My eyes followed her voice. More news? "Good or bad?" After all that had happened, I was a bit skittish about any kind of news. "Please, say it's good."

Eva laughed. "You may want to sit for this one." Uh-oh. What was going on? "Remember when I told you I was dating this guy?" I nodded. She'd said at the time that they hadn't known each other for very long. "Well, it got rather serious and…." She paused, and my heart stopped with her.

"What? What happened?"

My sister sighed and then giggled quietly. "Well… Oliver, I'm pregnant. You're going to be an uncle."

I froze, my jaws falling apart and my eyebrows shooting upwards. "Pregnant?" My sister had never seemed like the kind who one day would be a mother. Strange how things worked out sometimes. Even stranger, she seemed to be truly happy about it. "And you're glad?"

She now laughed in earnest. "Yes, Oliver. I'm very happy. I know I'm not the typical mommy kind, but I love Jack and I couldn't be happier I'm having his baby."

"Jack? Jack Thornton? My divorce lawyer?" Had they been meeting in secret all this time? I was shocked. In a good way. Jack was one of the good ones. A dying breed, it appeared.

Eva held my good hand, still wrapped around the papers. "Yes, that Jack. I started dating him about the time of your surgery, right before you lost your sight." It made sense. With me lying in a hospital bed and later blind, Eva had taken it upon herself to do all the legal legwork for my divorce. "I love him, Oliver, and we will be getting married soon. I wanted you to be the first one to know. Are you mad?"

"Why would I be mad? I'm so happy for you." Things were coming together, both for my sister and me. A lifetime of dysfunctional love was finally becoming a memory for the two of us. Nothing else. "I can't believe I'm going to be an uncle."

MARCY

I couldn't lie. I was a nervous wreck. Whatever possessed Oliver's father to invite me for a dinner at Chez Nicola was beyond me, and I was not about to speculate. Unless he had had a change of heart and was planning some kind of surprise celebration for his son's safe return from his adventure in the mountains? Which I somehow doubted. When his voice reached my ear from the other end of the line a few days before, you could have blown me over with a feather. Our last meeting at dinner had not left much doubt as to how he felt about me and my relationship with his son. What could he possibly want from me?

I squirmed in my seat the restaurant owner and chef had kindly led me to after finding out I was Oliver's girlfriend. "*Monsieur* Dawson is one of my favorite customers. He comes here with his sister all the time," the Frenchman had told me after placing a huge dish of delicious-looking chocolates in front of me. "Are you expecting him?"

"No, I'm meeting with Oliver's father, Mr. Dawson." I scanned the room again, looking for him but he was nowhere to be found. "Have you seen him?"

It turned out Nicola had never met the older Dawson. So, this was not one of his usual spots. Was he meeting me here so he was not seen with me by one of his associates? Whatever the reason was, the more I waited, the more nervous I was about the whole thing. I was almost ready to get up and leave when someone sat across from me.

"Ms. Spellman." The perfect, yet unpleasant face of Oliver's father offered me what he undoubtedly thought to be a fetching smile. With a flourish, he unrolled the napkin and placed it on his lap. "Thank you for coming."

I smiled nervously. "Sure. I admit, I'm a little curious as to why you wanted to talk to me." Why did he look like he had tasted a lemon? "Are you planning a surprise party for your son?"

He frowned. "What? What made you think that?" *The fact that you told me not to tell Oliver about this.* "I'll be quick. We want you to stop seeing my son."

If I hadn't been sitting, I probably would have fallen on my butt. What the hell? What made him think he could demand such a thing from me? "You want what? Why?"

"You're not the right girl for our boy." Why was he using the royal *we*? He must have a grand opinion of himself. "People like you are a detriment to those who excel in society. By attaching himself to someone like you, Oliver is hurting his chances at success and also hurting us, his family."

Bristling like a cat under attack, I leaned slightly over the table and lowered my voice. "Your *boy* is a man who knows what he wants and is plenty successful without your help." I touched the protection amulet around my neck. "I'm not leaving your son. I love him and I will stay by his side no matter what. For as long as he wants me."

"You're not good enough for him." His voice, like a growl dripping in contempt, made me shiver.

"Compared to what?" My voice went up a few octaves, and I noticed several curious glances in our direction. "Compared to the killer you pushed at him? The murderer whom you did everything in your power to protect?"

He waved his hand in front of him. "Quiet down. People are staring at us." He looked anxiously around us, but people had already lost interest. "If you don't stop seeing my son I will make sure his career in the police force will end quite abruptly. We never supported his choice to become a detective, but—"

I couldn't believe my own ears. "Are you threatening to hurt your own son's career to get what you want? To keep him lonely and unhappy?" My fists were closed so tightly my knuckles were turning purple. "How can you be so horrible?"

"We're only trying to protect Oliver from the likes of you."

"The likes of me are not the ones trying to kill him or make his life a living hell." My voice attracted the attention of a few people close by, and I made myself take a deep breath and lower my voice.

"Is everything all right?" It was Nicola, his brow creased with worry.

"Thank you, *Monsieur* Nicola, but I'm okay." He walked away, throwing glances at our table all the way to the kitchen. I turned to Oliver's father again, schooling myself to keep calm. "You say you're trying to protect him. Where were you when he needed protection from Blake?"

His mouth settled in a rigid line, and for all his handsome perfection the older Dawson suddenly looked haggard and ancient. "Think whatever you please, Miss Spellman. But if you love our son like you say you do, then you must leave him or he will lose the one thing he cares the most about, his job as a detective." I could hear the finality in his words and I believed him. He would sooner destroy his son's life than allow him to mix with me.

Slowly he stood up and looked at me one last time, icy eyes sharp as knives. "And do it now. Like a Band-Aid. It's better for everyone involved." Throwing the napkin on the table, he turned around and left. I was shaking in anger and frustration. What was I to do? Oliver did love that job better than anything else in life. Could I challenge his father and risk losing it for him? Could I be that selfish? Would I be able to live with myself knowing I was the reason for his misery?

I'm not sure how long I sat at that table, eyes burning with unshed tears, shaking like a leaf. Twice, Nicola came to check on me and twice I told him I was okay. I wasn't. Far from it. My heart was destroyed because no matter what I chose to do, in the end it would be the wrong choice.

I called Celia, my go-to in emergencies like this.

"He did what?" Celia placed a hand on her heart, her mouth opening wide. "You've got to be kidding. What kind of father is he?"

"I guess the kind that almost makes me happy I'm an orphan." Almost. My father may have died too early, but he was a good, loving dad and I would always carry him in my heart. "I don't know what to do, Celia."

Celia raised an eyebrow. "What do you mean? You're not actually considering doing what he asked you, are you?"

I hugged myself, my stomach tied in a million knots. "What else am I supposed to do? I can't have Oliver lose his job over this. I would never forgive myself. That job is his life." This was an impossible choice.

"How can you even consider leaving him?" Celia's outraged voice echoed through the store where we had met after I called her. "You love him. He loves you. I think the choice is clear." Clear as mud, maybe.

I covered my eyes with my hands and whimpered. "Oh Celia, what am I going to do?" Celia pulled me to her in a hug and I finally freed the tears that burned in my eyes. "I don't know what to do."

My friend stayed for a while and, after I closed the store, she drove with me to my place. "You're sure you don't want me to come in and stay the night? I can call Marc and tell him I'm not coming home. He'll understand."

I shook my head and pushed my glasses up with a finger. "I'll be okay. You go home and rest. You're working the early shift at the hospital, you need your rest." Reluctantly she waved and left me. I stood and stared at the closed door for God knew how long. Even if I wanted to, I wouldn't be able to recall any of my thoughts at the time. My mind had gone blank, as if my conversation with the senior Dawson had broken my brain and left an empty vacuum.

The strident ring of my phone woke me up from the trance. I dug through the myriad of stuff I carried in my purse to find it, but then I wished I hadn't. The caller ID displayed Oliver's name and number. I stared at the phone with my heart racing a million miles a second, listening to its ear-splitting rings, blinking every time the ringing stopped only to start again shortly after. My whole being craved to hear Oliver's soothing and sexy voice, the promise of another night in his arms, the hope of a lifetime in his heart. Instead I stood with the phone in the palm of my hand, ringing and vibrating in a wordless plea, waiting for it to stop for good. I had made my decision. I wouldn't be the one destroying Oliver's beloved career.

Nosy Chefs & Blind Magic

OLIVER

"You got to be shitting me." Marc sounded so annoyed I could imagine him, his mouth all scrunched up into a frown. "Why? Did she tell you why?"

"She's not even talking to me at all, Marc." Marcy hadn't called or come to see me in over a week. When I tried to go see her at the store, Eva and I found a notice at the door saying the store was closed because of a family emergency. I was hoping that Marc could shed some light on the mysterious and sudden absence of my little witch, but he seemed as surprised by it all as I was.

"Celia hasn't mentioned anything." He hissed, this funny whistling noise he made when he was puzzled by something. "But she has been acting a little weird, even for her. I bet she knows something and she's not talking. You know women, if you don't ask them directly they just think we already know." I heard his chair move. "I'm going home right now and I will find out, my friend. You can count on me." I knew I could.

Eva came to pick me up from work that evening. "We're having dinner at Chez Nicola." I opened my mouth to protest. "I don't want to hear a word from you. We're going and that's that. You need some good food and some company."

There would be no point in arguing with my sister. She had inherited my father's stubbornness and I knew she wouldn't back down. Unlike my father, though, Eva used her trait for good. I put on my jacket, straightened my tie out of habit, and left with her. Looping my good arm through hers, I walked across the precinct main hall, my head down. My blindness didn't protect me from feeling the stares of my coworkers, who were all too aware of Marcy's sudden disappearance from my life.

I had asked a friend in the force to discreetly check on Marcy, and I knew she was in good health. In fact, nothing seemed to be wrong with my beautiful little witch. That left me with one unpleasant conclusion: Marcy didn't want me in her life anymore. Had I scared her with my rather intense and quick declaration of love? She hadn't seemed too at ease with the idea at first. I couldn't help but notice how reluctant she was to tell me she loved me, too. Maybe it had been too much, too fast for her.

At the restaurant, Eva requested a more private booth. Nicola himself brought us bread and butter and a bottle of their best wine on the house. I must have reeked heartbreak if everybody around me was going out of their way to be so nice. I sighed, half-resigned to be the object of all that pity; the poor blind guy who was jilted by his girlfriend.

"Oliver, you must take better care of yourself." Eva poured us some wine and the fruity smell made me wish I was the type to drink my troubles away. "You look disheveled, and look at that sling. It's all crooked and barely supporting your arm."

"I'm going to the doctor in two days. I don't need this sling anymore." At least that's what I hoped. It had been over a month since the surgery, and I was very tired of having my arm hang from my neck like that. "And I'm just tired that's all."

"Have you been sleeping at all?" I took a sip of the wine and put down the glass. Even my taste buds refused to rejoice.

"Not much." Why lie? She could see straight through me. "I think I may be suffering from Non-24-Hour Sleep-Wake disorder." I didn't believe it for a minute. I knew why I wasn't sleeping well. Marcy had ripped my heart apart without even telling me why. She was constantly in my thoughts, my dreams… I craved her like some people craved drink or drugs. I needed her in my life. She was my balance, my magic potion for happiness.

"You're not sleeping because of Marcy." I knew I couldn't fool her. "I'm going over there today and asking her why she stopped seeing you."

"I may know why." I was surprised by the voice of Nicola. Had he been listening to our conversation? The man had no filter. "I apologize for overhearing your conversation, but…." The French-accented voice hesitated. "Your girlfriend, the pretty red-haired one, was here a week or so ago having dinner with your father."

That got my attention. Marcy and my father? Together? "What do you mean?"

The Frenchman cleared his throat. "I didn't even know it was your father, Mr. Dawson, until Ms. Spellman told me. *Mais oui*, they were here for a very short time a couple weeks ago."

I heard a chair scratch the floors. "Sit with us, *Monsieur* Nicola, please," Eva said.

"I didn't think any of it until I overheard what he was saying to the young *mademoiselle*." The chef sounded embarrassed to admit he had been eavesdropping on his customers. "I heard your father order her to stop seeing you."

A rock fell into my stomach. "He did what?"

"*Monsieur* Dawson told *la mademoiselle* that if she didn't stop seeing you, he would make sure your career as a *détective* was over."

My sister let out a gasp. "You've got to be kidding! He threatened her?"

"*Oui*, he told her your future lay in her hands and left without even ordering any food." The French chef's outrage at such a breach of restaurant etiquette was obvious. "Poor *mademoiselle* sat there for the longest time, her eyes red with tears. I checked on her a couple times but I didn't know what else to do."

I couldn't talk. My vocal chords seemed paralyzed by

the anger I felt toward my father. Eva came to the rescue. "Thank you so much, *Monsieur* Nicola. We appreciate your candor. This explains a lot."

The chef apologized again for overhearing our conversation, and went back to work. I still couldn't speak, anger burning red in my chest. I clenched my jaws so hard my teeth hurt. I was going to kill him.

"I don't know what to say, Oliver." My sister's subdued voice was shaken. "I keep hoping that Father sees the error of his ways, but it seems my faith is misplaced. What do you want to do?"

I may have growled. "Take me to Marcy's place."

Soon enough I was standing at her door, ringing the bell and knocking so hard several of her neighbors came to check on it. My sister put their minds to rest and I resumed.

"Open this freaking door, Marcy!" I didn't want to scare her off by screaming, but I was so angry. Not at her. Well, maybe a little mad at her, but mostly at my father and his irrational need to control everything in my life. "I know about my father, Marcy. Please…." I leaned forward, my forehead resting on the cool wood of the door. My voice shook with emotion. "Please, little witch. Talk to me. Please."

The door creaked and slowly opened. I could see Marcy's red hair, like a fiery explosion of color, and my anger immediately faded into the background. I took a step toward her and wrapped her in a one-arm hug. "God, I missed you." Her lavender scent soothed my nerves as I covered her in a million little kisses.

"I'll leave the two of you alone," my sister said. "I'll be in the car if you need me. I have a phone call to make."

Marcy closed the door behind us and without a word, she led me to the couch. She sat next to me and I brushed my fingers across her cheeks. She was crying. "Don't cry, Marcy." I drew her into an embrace. "My father is the cruelest man you will ever meet. I never shared this with you, but he has made my life miserable from the time I was born and he hasn't stopped yet."

Everything came spilling out. All the secrets I had kept even from myself about the years of physical and emotional abuse I had suffered at the hands of my father. It was embarrassing for me, as a man, to admit to having been putty in the hands of my cruel father and to still today have nightmares about it. How I had felt helpless and hopeless for so long, and how even after becoming independent from him, he still plagued my life in so many ways. How stupid I felt for always hoping things would get better, that one day my father would be proud of me and apologize for what he had done.

"So, you see we can't give in to his threats. We can't allow him to control my life anymore."

"But he will get you fired." Marcy hiccupped, tears still rolling down her cheeks onto my shoulder where she rested her head.

"No, he won't." He would try for sure, but just like he had friends in high places, I had friends that believed in me and trusted me. "And if he does, it's not the end of the world."

"But you love that job." Marcy's voice caught again, and I yearned to cover her mouth with mine and kiss her until she smiled again. "It's your life. It's what you love the most in the world."

I chuckled. "Sweet witch, I do love my job and maybe at some point it was the one thing I loved the most. But not anymore." Marcy's head left my shoulder and her hand touched my face in a small caress that sent shivers down my spine. "The one thing I love the most in life now is you, little witch. You are my life."

I felt her mouth on mine before I was finished talking. Her tantalizing sweetness seeped between my lips to mingle with my tongue in a dance that sent me spiraling into bliss. I moaned into her mouth. It had only been a couple of weeks, but it felt like an eternity without her touch, without her flavor. My broken arm itched to escape the sling and wrap itself around my little witch.

"Don't even think about it." Marcy slid my jacket off my shoulders. "I'll do the work." Carefully she undid the sling so she could slip my shirt off, and then spread her hands across my chest, over my heart. "Are you saying your heart is mine now?" I nodded, too turned on to talk.

Marcy held my good hand and brought it to her chest. "Mine is yours." I felt her fingers work the buttons on her shirt, and a few moments later her naked, warm skin was under my palm. Intoxicated by the way she felt, I leaned over and searched for her breast with my lips. Filled with irrational glee, I realized she wasn't wearing a bra. While my mouth and tongue played with her senses, I hooked my arm around her waist and picked her up. Her legs went around my waist, bracing her while I carried her to… I had no idea where the bed was. I groaned, frustrated.

"To your left. I'll guide you." Marcy blew her words softly into my ear and I shivered. Following her lead, I found my way to the bed and laid her gently on top. A pull on my pants told me Marcy was undressing me, her hand skimming the fabric over my hardness. I swelled further. She giggled. "Slow down, Oliver. We still have some layers of clothing to get rid of."

When we were finally both naked, I swept my hand from her neck all the way down her body, reveling in her silkiness, her warmth. "I love how you feel, little witch." My hand brushed between her legs and a shiver of pleasure ran through me when she whimpered and arched against my fingers. "Don't ever doubt I love you more than anything else in life."

"I love you, Oliver." Marcy sat up suddenly and glued herself to me, bringing her hands around to flatten them on my buttocks, pressing me harder against her. "Don't you ever forget that."

"Or what? You'll put a hex on me?" I laughed against her mouth, heady with her scent and feel.

"Too late for that." She giggled, her tongue flickering over my lips. "I already did."

MARCY

"Man, this looks like a tomb." The store was drowned in darkness, which was weird because I always left some lights on. Oliver, right behind me, felt his way in with the cane and closed the door behind him. I went for the light switch and flicked it upwards.

As the light flooded the space, familiar faces popped from behind the counter. "Surprise!" Polka-dot balloons and streamers flew everywhere, and a huge banner on the wall behind the counter read: Happy Birthday to the Best Witch in the World. Tears immediately came up to my eyes. I was so emotional lately.

From behind, Oliver crossed his arms—both of them, since he had been promoted to a simple, flexible cast— in front of me, squeezing me tight against him. "Happy birthday, little witch." The tears did roll down then, fast and furious, pooling around my mouth and fogging up my glasses. "You're very loved, Marcy."

Emily Rose, hand in hand with her future husband, Jem, stepped forward and enveloped me in a hug. "You have been such a good friend to Celia and us. We'll never forget what you did for us when we were in danger. Happy birthday, sweetie."

All six-odd feet of Jem joined in the hug. He chuckled. "Yeah, even though you tried to knock me out with one of your potions, I still love you."

"In all fairness, I was doing it at your fiancée's request." I tried to wipe my tears and managed to make a huge mess of my makeup instead, mascara staining my fingers and undoubtedly my face as well. We laughed. Well, I snorted, fishing a tissue out of my pocket to clean my snotty nose.

Celia jumped in and forcibly pushed Jem out of the way. "She's my friend. You don't get to hug her before I do." I snorted again and hung from her neck. "Happy birthday, my friend. I made your favorite cake." I pulled back and looked at her suspiciously. "Okay, I didn't actually make it. But I did order it from your favorite bakery." I laughed and hugged her again.

"Let's get this party started, then." Eva stepped from behind the counter, her classic beauty almost glistening against the dark background. Placing a hand on my shoulder, Oliver's sister smiled. "My brother got a good one this time." For some reason that simple comment filled me with such joy I almost cried again.

Polka Dots & Eye of Newt had never seen such festivities. My birthday party rolled through the evening into the night. Celia had organized a catered dinner and set some makeshift tables with pretty polka-dot tablecloths. Oliver sat with me and Eva while we munched on the delicious chocolate cake Celia had ordered from my favorite bakery.

"I must admit I'm surprised your father didn't make good on his threats." Dumbfounded was a more appropriate word to describe what I felt. I had been more than certain Oliver Dawson Sr. would go through with his promise of making his son's career a thing of the past.

Eva looked at her brother and I noticed a little smile dancing in the corners of her mouth. "Well, he was going to but I convinced him otherwise."

Oliver laughed. "She did more than convince him. I think he will be out of our lives for good."

I looked at Eva, my eyebrow raised. "What did you do exactly?"

"I reminded my father that I knew about his involvement with Blake for the last ten years and that I would be more than glad to leak that information to the press should he insist on giving you guys a hard time. And I could always add a story or two about how he abused my brother." Eva took a dainty bite of the chocolate deliciousness. "In case people doubt my word against his, I'm sure I could persuade the hospital staff to testify to the way he acted when Oliver was shot." She smiled. "I think he got the idea."

"If the local press got wind of his close relationship with Blake—and the way he treated me as a child—his reputation would be destroyed and so would his status as the lawyer to the rich and politically famous," Oliver explained, his hand seeking mine on top of the table. "The one thing my father loves more than life itself." I understood now. The one thing that would stop the monster who had fathered these two beautiful individuals was the same motivating his ill-doing.

Someone—I suspected Celia, who was already entwined in Marc's strong arms—had put on some music, and my pink stiletto heels were tapping to the beat. "Want to dance, Oliver?" I had never seen my sweet man dance but the idea of having him flush against me, moving slowly to the seductive tune, was too enticing to resist.

Oliver raised his eyebrows and the corner of his lips curled. "Me? Dancing?" He chuckled softly. "In case you have missed it, I'm blind."

I had already jumped to my feet and was tugging on his hand. "What does that have anything to do with dancing? Are you making excuses because you're a dreadful dancer?"

He swiped a hand across his mouth and caught his lower lip between his teeth. "*Au contraire*, my sweet witch. I've been told I'm as smooth on the dance floor as Fred Astaire."

It was my turn to laugh. "Right. And I'm Ginger Rogers!" With a last, more forcible tug I pulled him to his feet.

"You have the hair to match the name." Swiftly he twirled me around until I crashed none too gently into his chest. "Ouch! But obviously not the skill." I slapped him playfully and allowed myself to be cocooned by his warm, familiar arms. My head rested on his hard, welcoming chest and we swayed to the languorous music. We were in no hurry now. For the first time since we had met, I felt calm and secure in the knowledge Oliver loved me. And better yet, *I* loved him back. Deeply.

OLIVER

"Earth, air, fire, sea, let the goddess's love shine through me!" I could hear her quiet chanting from the bathroom over the sound of running water as I woke up. Was she doing one of her spells? I smiled, a feeling of contentment warming me up from the inside as I stretched like a lazy cat on my bed. Marcy spent most of her nights at my place now, her scent clinging to every object I owned, reminding me how much I loved that little woman.

"Let him love me and I him with all the strength of our hearts." What was she doing? Too curious to sit and do nothing, I swung my legs over the side of the bed and searched for my cane. I walked as quietly as I could, hoping she wouldn't hear the click-clack of metal feeling its way across the wooden floor.

The smell of lavender and rose wafted to my nose as I approached the bathroom door. I inhaled deeply and closed my eyes. I didn't know whether I would ever be able to see again, but Marcy had infused my darkness with such color and light, I often forgot I was blind. Hers was a world of scents, tastes, and textures, which she willingly and unselfishly shared with me every day.

As stealthily as I could, I slowly pushed the door open and stood under the doorframe, listening to the soothing sound of Marcy's soft voice chanting one of her spells. "Let our love grow and strengthen." I smiled like a fool, my heart overflowing with the kind of love I always hoped I'd feel but never had before.

"Jesus! Oliver!" Her sudden screech made me laugh. "Don't laugh. You scared the bejesus out of me. I thought you were asleep."

Stepping inside the bathroom, I followed her voice and came to a stop when my cane hit the edge of the bathtub. "Are you taking a bath?" I could smell the subtle scent of candles burning. "Can I join you?"

A big splash of water was followed by some sloshing, and before I knew it I had a very wet and naked Marcy attached to me. Her hands flattened against my bare chest,

Marcy trembled. "I'm here." Her breath caressed my lips and it was my turn to shiver.

I felt next to me for the towel I knew was hanging there, and in a wide swoop, I unfolded it over Marcy's back all the way to my chest and pulled her closer. "You're shivering."

Her giggle sounded like metal hitting crystal. A clear, pure vibration that made me mushy inside. "Not from cold." Her lips connected with mine and teased them open. Not that it took much coaxing for me to open up to her. I drank her in and my arms closed around her even tighter.

"What were you doing, little witch? Putting another hex on me? You know I'm already hooked, right?"

Her hands, caught between me and her breasts, were wet and warm, covering my skin with a delicious tingling. "It's a spell for strengthening our relationship." I kissed that little spot right behind her ear and she whimpered a little. "So that nothing will come between the two of us."

"No force on earth will take me away from you, girl." I placed a short trail of kisses along her cheeks and chin. "I love you, Marcy." My voice was hoarse from desire. Being close to Marcy was the most exhilarating feeling I had ever had, and my body responded to her at the slightest provocation. If I didn't know any better, I would believe she had me indeed under some kind of spell.

"Can I finish the incantation?" How could I say no? What I really wanted was to pick her up, take her to my bed, and make her mine again. But I nodded instead. Marcy planted a kiss in the center of my chest. "Let him love me and I him with all the strength of our hearts. Let our love grow and strengthen. Earth, air, fire, sea, let the goddess's love shine through me."

In spite of it all, I found myself repeating those words and believing it. I wanted our love to grow. I wanted it to get stronger. "I love you, little witch." Silence fell and I could hear the water dripping slowly from the faucet and the soft crackling of the candles. Marcy's naked body against me was playing havoc with my senses. "Is it done?"

"Why the hurry?" Her hands had freed themselves and were now feeling their way along my back and sliding under the waist of my very wet pants. "Should I get rid of them? Your pants?" She moved against me and I gasped at the surge of yearning and pleasure the simple movement caused.

"Shit, Marcy. This is torture." The good kind, of course.

"Do I have to do it all by myself?" She didn't have to ask twice. I went to work on loosening up the laces on my pajama pants and, in no time, we achieved utter bareness. "Love this."

My eyebrows shot up. "The sex?"

She slapped my arm and laughed. "No, dummy—even though it *is* awesome. I'm talking about the intimacy, us being here. Bare, body and soul, nothing between us. It makes me twinkle inside."

I kissed her, relishing her flavor, her heat. God, I was so freaking in love with this little woman. We had been together now for almost six months, and I couldn't wait to see what the future brought us. "I was not going to do this until our half-year anniversary, but I can't stand it anymore." I picked her up in my arms and walked toward the bed, hoping I wouldn't lose my sense of direction and crash into something. I laid her down on the bed, brushing a hand over her body from her neck to her thigh. There was something I needed from the nightstand and for once it was not a condom.

"What in heaven's name are you doing?" I had turned my back to her while I searched through the small drawer with both hands. With the tiny object hidden inside my hand, I turned around to Marcy and held her hand. "What's going on? I thought we were going to make love."

"Oh, we are most definitely going to make love." I realized I was nervous. What was I afraid of? Even though I couldn't be sure, I was pretty secure in the knowledge my little witch loved me as much as I loved her. "But first there is something I need to do."

Judging by her silence, Marcy was intrigued and waiting. I looked at her, her fiery red hair invading the darkness of my eyes. "Sweet little witch, would you do me the honor of being my wife?" We hadn't known each other for very long, but after all we had gone through together I felt we had already had a lifetime of togetherness. We knew each other better than most couples did after years of being together. I was ready. But was she? "It doesn't have to be soon, if you're not ready. But sometime in the future. I want to grow old with you. I want to be able to love you forever."

The silence was nerve-racking. For the first time in a long time, I hated not being able to see. What was the expression on her face? What was she thinking? Then it hit me. I knew she was smiling. "Well, are you going to make a blind man suffer?"

I felt her arms go around my neck and her legs wrapping themselves around my waist as she climbed on my lap. "Do you have a ring? You know a girl can't say yes until she sees that rock." She giggled against my lips, her face wet with tears.

Inside my hand, the ring my sister had helped me buy a week ago dug into the skin of my palm. I opened it between us. "Will this one do? Eva assured me you'd love it." She shrieked and I laughed. "I guess that's a yes."

Marcy pulled my face to her and kissed me, her tears of joy seeping between our lips, their saltiness mixed with the sweetness of her taste. "Yes, yes. I will marry you. Tomorrow, next year, whenever. I love you, Oliver Dawson, I love you."

Later that morning, as we lay side by side in the afterglow of love, I turned to Marcy, her head on my shoulder and her soft, wild hair tickling the side of my face. "There is one thing I must know, little witch."

"Yes?"

"What kind of love hex did you use on me?" She didn't answer right away, but I could tell, without actually seeing it, she had a little wicked smile on her lips and a twinkle in her eyes.

"Blind magic, sweetheart. Plain, blind magic."

Acknowledgments

This is the part where I panic for fear of forgetting to thank someone deserving of my ever-lasting gratitude.

Marcy's story would not have happened if it weren't for the insistence and enthusiasm of readers who wanted to know more about this character. Thank you. The little witch is now my favorite character so far.

My sister's interest in everything magical inspired me to write Marcy in the first place, so thanks, sis. All those teen years we spent, messing around with tarot cards and reading about crystals, came in handy for this story.

I'm lucky to be part of an online community of writers and readers who have supported me and cheered me on even when I felt like giving up. Too many to name, but a big heartfelt thank you goes to all of you.

My editors, Liv, Barbara, and Peggy, who made me feel like a million bucks with their comments and didn't hate me for my preposition-impairment. You rock!

My amazing publisher, Becky, who believed in me and my writing. She has been an inspiration, and I want to be like her when I grow up.

My friend and redhead, Tammie, who beta read this book and helped me find what was missing. Thank you for your honesty and enthusiasm.

Thank you to my three most faithful readers, Kathy, Ann-Marie, and Jean. You guys have been awesome.

And finally, to my family both here in the US and in Portugal, a great big thank-you for encouraging and supporting me in this crazy journey. Love you always.

About the Author

Natalina wrote her first romance in collaboration with her best friend at the age of 13. Since then she has ventured into other genres, but romance is first and foremost in almost everything she writes. Her novel, We Will Always Have the Closet, is her first published romance.

After earning a degree in tourism and foreign languages, she worked as a tourist guide in her native country, Portugal, for a short time before moving to the United States. She's lived in three continents and a few islands, and her knack for languages and linguistics led her to a master's degree in education. She lives in Virginia where she has taught English as a second language to elementary school children for more years than she cares to admit.

Natalina doesn't believe you can have too many books or too much coffee. Art and dance make her happy and she is pretty sure she could survive on lobster and bananas alone. When she is not writing or stressing over lesson plans, she shares her life with her husband and two adult sons.

You can reach out to Natalina at the following places:
FACEBOOK: WWW.FACEBOOK.COM/AUTHORNATALINAREIS
WEBSITE: WWW.CATARINADEOBIDOS.WORDPRESS.COM
TWITTER: WWW.TWITTER.COM/TICHAB

About the Publisher

Hot Tree Publishing opened its doors in 2015 with an aspiration to bring quality fiction to the world of readers. With the initial focus on romance and a wide spread of romance sub-genres, we envision opening up to alternative genres in the near future.

Firmly seated in the industry as a leading editing provider to independent authors and small publishing houses, Hot Tree Publishing is the sister company to Hot Tree Editing, founded in 2012. Having established in-house editing and promotions, plus having a well-respected market presence, Hot Tree Publishing endeavors to be a leader in bringing quality stories to the world of readers.

Interested in discovering more amazing reads brought to you by Hot Tree Publishing or perhaps you're interested in submitting a manuscript and joining the HTPubs family? Either way, head over to the website for information:

WWW.HOTTREEPUBLISHING.COM